THE RISE OF THE WILD CARDS

THE RISE OF THE WILD CARDS

by Nirav Udupa

DALLAS GRAHAM, INC.
SALT LAKE CITY 2022

First printing, 2022.

This book was printed on-demand, limiting its carbon footprint,
saving on unnecessary storage, and avoiding production waste.

If you decide to part with this book, do so responsibly:
please repurpose with a bookseller in your community.

ISBN 978-1-7345232-9-4
LCCN 2022939319

Copy edited by Annabelle Clawson Richards
Cover illustration by Grace Flynn
Book design by Dallas Graham

dallasgrahaminc.com

This book was made possible through the happy collaboration between
Make-A-Wish Greater Bay Area and the Red Fred Project.

ACKNOWLEDGEMENTS

I want to acknowledge everyone who has helped me create my book, especially those who have helped me during my cancer.

First, a huge thanks to everyone at Make-A-Wish Greater Bay Area. I am able to achieve my dream of becoming an author because of them. I also want to thank Dallas Graham for helping me while I was writing; his encouragement was helpful; he was the best mentor/editor I could ask for. A big thanks to my parents, Shital and Ratish Udupa, for their unlimited belief and support. Thanks to my brother, Dhruv Udupa, for being a constant for me during my time with cancer. He took care of himself and stayed strong when my parents were not able to be with him a lot of the time. A big thanks to my extended family—I'm grateful they want to read my book! Thanks to all my teachers, too, for their support and belief. Thanks to my dog, Polo, for cheering me up. (He was a great gift after cancer.) A special thanks to Grace Flynn for illustrating the cover and the different editors who helped my book take shape throughout all my writring.

I also want to thank all of my family and friends who have been waiting to read the book and have committed to buying a copy! It's finally here! Lastly, thanks to a few of my friends who have helped me out in the process of making my book. It meant a lot.

Nirav Udupa

RED FRED PROJECT

A story doesn't breathe until we hear it.
A book doesn't live until we read it.

The Red Fred Project was created to amplify the voices and minds and spirits of children living in extraordinary circumstances through original stories that turned into illustrated children's books. Each of our selected child-authors lives with a rare disease or life-threatening illness. But as you know and I know and the author of *this* book knows: these children are not simply patients—and they certainly are not defined by the unique physical challenges they face every day. These children are *storytellers*. And *authors!* And if we adults can sit still long enough and listen softly enough, we will realize these magnificent beings are our *teachers*, too.

I was thrilled when Ana Maria Vallarino contacted me and asked if I could assist her granting a wish for a talented and determined young man living in California. "He wants to publish his first novel. Can you help us?"

From the very first day Nirav and I met via Zoom conference call, I never stopped smiling. His attitude and imagination were infectious, and always left me inspired—wanting to do better, be better. But not just a better storyteller or writer; I wanted to be a better *person*, too. He's done the unbelieveable, the Herculean: *while* overcoming the daily rigors that come with cancer, he wrote a mystery novel! How many of you have done that?

I'm proud of you, Nirav. Very proud. And I'm forever grateful to Make-A-Wish for allowing me to work alongside you. This is just the beginning of your incredible life. Keep making the world a better place through your mind, your ideas, your stories, your words, and your giant heart.

Congratulations! Don't stop, buddy.
Dallas Graham, Founder & Publisher
Red Fred Project

MAKE-A-WISH

Since 1984, Make-A-Wish Greater Bay Area has granted more than 9,000 life-changing wishes for children with critical illnesses who live as far south as Monterey County and as far north as the Oregon border. Every one of those wishes has a beautiful story. In Nirav's case, his wish was to create a beautiful story.

As an avid lover of mystery, it's been my pleasure to follow the twists and turns as the plot of Nirav's wish has unfolded over the past year. While Nirav is the creative mastermind behind this magnum opus, many supporting characters played instrumental parts in the process. Our wish planner, Ana Maria Vallarino, has my deepest gratitude for expertly stewarding this wish from the opening sentence to the final page. I'd also like to thank Dallas Graham from the Red Fred Project for his dedicated support of Nirav as a writing mentor throughout his creative process and for stewarding the novel through publication.

Most of all, thank you to Nirav for allowing us to be a part of writing a chapter in your beautiful story, and for being a part of ours. Although a good mystery must be solved and come to a satisfying close, the best part about the Make-A-Wish story is that there's never an ending. We always have more to write, read, and time to enjoy with our favorite characters—the wish children and families we serve.

Best wishes,
Betsy Biern, CEO
Make-A-Wish Greater Bay Area

CHAPTERS

CHAPTER 1

GIRL

It was midnight, and Silvis Wren couldn't sleep. But it wasn't the crashing thunder outside his window that kept him awake, curled up in a ball at the bottom of his bed. It was Polo. He was missing.

"Where are you, Polo? Where are you?" Silvis moaned, exhausted from worrying. Ugh, try searching the house again, you worrywart.

Silvis sat up, stretched, and scuffled out of the basement and into the kitchen. Lightning flashed outside the window. He was still hungry, so he scarfed down some potato chips lying on the counter.

"C'mon, Polo! Where are you? You better not be trying to scare me!" he yelled between crunches.

A shuffling sound came from the stairs. Silvis bit into another chip and investigated, but there was nothing to see. He looked around the hallways, too—rushed through all the rooms (again!)—but still, no signs of Polo. Retracing his steps one more time, he stopped. How did I forget the attic?

It was still summertime, so the room would be humid, even at night. It's unlikely, with the heat, but Polo is a crazy ape. Silvis made his way to the middle of the hallway and pulled the rope from the ceiling, connected to the ladder. Once it was down, he climbed up and was hit by a wave of the attic's warm summer breath. "Ooo-wee!" he said.

He continued until he reached the top and then he flipped a switch. One measly light flickered awake. The floorboards creaked while he ducked around old cardboard boxes, calling out, "Polo? Polo?"

Just then, he heard a scattering noise. Silvis rushed toward the sound and caught Polo trying to hide behind a tower of cardboard boxes, holding Silvis's computer!

"Polo! Get back here!"

The furry ape didn't pay him any attention; he just ran until he found a darkened corner behind a rocking horse.

Silvis snuck up on him and seized his arm. The ape jumped. "You gave me a heart attack, Polo! I thought you left the house. Bad ape! And what are you doing with my computer?!"

"Sorry," Polo motioned with his hands.

Silvis didn't know how—or why—his missing parents had taught Polo sign language, but it was helpful for these moments.

Silvis grabbed the computer from Polo and checked the screen for damage, but all he saw were scripts and weird coding languages, as well as some hacked files that Polo was downloading.

"What did I tell you about hacking, Polo?"

"But it's helpful hacking."

"How?" asked Silvis.

"I figured out how to get you into school."

Silvis rolled his eyes. "Is this another one of your 'brilliant' plans?"

Polo frowned and put his head down. "Oh, I'm sorry, old boy. You must be serious. Okay. Tell me: what did you find out?"

Silvis had called Hillstretch Elementary probably 100 times, begging to be admitted, but the school wouldn't allow him to enroll—because he had no parents.

Polo smiled and started signing rapidly. "We're going to steal another student's registration card. There's a girl who's at the Hawkman's house a lot—probably his daughter."

The Hawkman was a creepy man in the neighborhood who looked like a hawk. All the kids were afraid of him and gave him that nickname because they didn't know his real name.

Polo continued, "We'll steal her card, and then I'll use it to register you online and create a fake card for you so you can get into the building." The ape smiled a big, silly grin.

Silvis smirked and shook his head. "At this point, I'll try anything. You sure about this—using the card to register and get into the school?"

"Of course!"

"Okay," said Silvis. "But don't tell anybody—ever—that I became a thief for one night just so I could go to school."

•

Thirty minutes later, they were outside the Hawkman's house. Polo's hairy back stuck out of the bush they were hiding behind. Silvis didn't think it was a problem until he spied someone in the Hawkman's house. "Get down!" he said, lowering his voice.

Polo ducked. The Hawkman stepped out of the house and got into his car. A couple minutes later, he drove away.

The boy and his ape waited a few more minutes. "We gotta be careful—and be quiet." Silvis tiptoed out of the bush, toward the Hawkman's house, while Polo clung onto his back. As they got close to the house, someone in a raincoat was approaching. Silvis ran behind two trash bins nearby.

"Phew!" Polo signed.

The raincoat-wearing person sat down beside a tree. It was a girl with short hair, dyed red at the top. She had a sparkle in her eyes, which made Polo think she was a little girl. This must be the Hawkman's daughter, Silvis thought.

"We have no other choice. We have to attack her, so she doesn't tell anybody we were here—in case she sees us. We can take her; she looks young," reasoned Polo.

"Are you crazy?! You watch too many action movies. No way! We're gonna have to sneak past her. I may be a thief for one night, but I'll never be a thug. Now, keep quiet."

While the girl was deeply distracted by her phone, Silvis crept out behind the two trash bins and crawled past the girl until he was blocked by the house. Staying low, he found a window that had been left open. He lifted it a little higher and Polo jumped from his back through the window. Silvis was getting ready to climb in, until...

"Hey!" the girl yelled.

Silvis's heart beat faster than ever and sweat poured down his head. He didn't dare to turn around. It's game over.

"I'm talking to you, boy! What are you doing? What do you want?!" the girl yelled, again.

Silvis didn't move.

"You're probably just one of the dumb boys from school who's too stupid to come up with an excuse for breaking into this house. You probably look at all the nerds' papers whenever you take a test because your brain can't remember the simplest things. You probably like to spread mean rumors, too. All boys do."

Silvis had had it with this girl—but he wasn't about to attack her. Slowly, he turned around and glowered. He didn't trust her; in fact, he didn't trust girls at all.

When the girl saw his face, she squinted.

Silvis waited a few seconds and then yelled, "You better scram before I teach you a lesson!"

"How could you teach anything when you're so stupid? All boys are idiots!" the girl yelled. "Wait ... you sound like that kid—! I'm gonna tell the Hawkman about you!" she yelled.

The girl ran at Silvis and threw a punch. Silvis ducked down and dodged surprisingly fast.

"Don't you mean your dad?!"

"He's not my dad, you idiot! I just work for him!" she screamed while she threw another blow.

"What can a girl your age and size do for work?" Silvis said.

The girl tossed off her raincoat and pushed her sleeves up. Silvis was surprised: the girl seemed like she was his age without the jacket on. She was wearing funky, spy, bandit-like clothes.

"Why are you so mysterious and why don't you go to school?" the girl sneered.

"So, you've been watching me? Better clear out or I'll tell the Hawkman that you've been spying on me," Silvis teased.

"No. I haven't been... I've never—"

"Yes you did; yes you have. And I'll have no problem telling the Hawkman."

"Fine! But, who are you? And why are you always alone?" she demanded.

Silvis wanted the conversation to end, immediately, so he decided to share his biggest secret. "I... uhh... I don't live with my parents. They disappeared a few years ago."

"Really? They're gone? What happened?" the girl said.

Silvis was about to say when suddenly—

Bang! Bong! Loud noises came from the open window.

"Hey! What's that noise?" the girl cried.

Just then, Polo hopped out of the open window, holding the card that would get Silvis into school.

"Drop that, you stupid ape!" she yelled.

"He's not vicious. In fact, he's super friendly and super smart. He can understand, ask questions, and obey—all in sign language."

"Okay, then tell him to give me back the card," she growled.

"Actually, I need the card. It's my only way to get into school."

"And why should I let you have it?"

"Because I really need to go to school, and with my parents gone, I don't have a chance. Except with your help. And your card."

The girl crossed her arms and rolled her eyes. "Okay. Fine. Take the card but give it back when you're done."

"Thanks," Silvis replied. "I really appreciate it."

Polo handed Silvis the card and they began to walk away.

"Hey, wait! What's your name, ape-boy?"

"Silvis. What about you?"

"You can call me Willow."

"Okay. Willow. Thanks again for letting us steal your card."

•

It was almost 2 A.M. when Silvis and Polo got home and figured out how to use the code associated with the card. Silvis carefully entered the code on the Hillstretch Elementary website. Like magic, all of Silvis's teachers, classmates, staff, and other useful information popped up. Polo then made Silvis a fake ID card. "This should work," he said, handing it to Silvis.

"Wow! I'm finally going to school! But how did the school assign me to all these classes in just a few seconds?" He puzzled on this until he walked into his bed across from Polo, who was already fast asleep.

CHAPTER 2

DETECTIVE

Silvis woke up early. He couldn't wait another minute to go to school. Most kids dreaded going to school. Not Silvis—he hadn't been since kindergarten and he could hardly remember anything that had happened then. Now, he was in fifth grade, and the golden, shining sun reflected his mood: *It's going to be a great day; I can just feel it! And if I can get Polo to calm down...*

Suddenly, he realized he hadn't made plans for an ape-sitter. Polo could be naughty, so leaving him at the house—alone—could be a big problem.

Silvis groaned while he tied his shoes. "What on earth are we gonna do with you?"

"Nothing," said Polo. "I'm fine staying home alone."

Silvis was out of time. School was starting soon, and the bus would be on his block any minute. "No, you're not," argued Silvis, "but I have no choice but to leave you here. Don't throw all of my clothes on the floor again."

Silvis pulled on his backpack, grabbed a cold breakfast burrito, and ran out the door—just in time to see the school bus arrive on Newburg Street. He knew he should be more worried about his ape, but the novelty of the yellow bus and the prospects of going to school made his worries fade away. Silvis skipped into the bus with a smile on his face. The kids on the bus didn't talk to him, but he didn't mind.

Once his bus arrived, he walked confidently towards the front gate. it was morning recess, so Silvis had some free time to walk around the school yard. He couldn't remember much from his days in kindergarten, the last time he went to school, except for a few ghost memories of him with his parents.

A large group of kids huddled together close by. Silvis joined the group. "What's going on here?" he asked.

"Shhh!" several kids hissed.

They were all staring at a kid setting up a stand, dressed as a detective in a full suit and tie. He had a pipe dangling out of his mouth that was blowing bubbles. That kid is doomed. Not the best choice of what to wear on the first day of school, thought Silvis.

The boy didn't seem to mind the others staring. By the time he was finished setting up his stand, he began handing out his service cards and lollipops, and he even had a tip can. But the most surprising thing was the professional sign he had set up:

DETECTIVE SERVICES FOR HIRE.

The crowd moved in.

The boy shifted his weight from side to side and said, "Hi. I'm J-Junior. I offer detective services."

To Silvis's surprise, no one snickered or laughed—just gave a couple of "whoas" and "wows." Junior turned his back to the group and went back to setting up his stand.

Silvis snuck up behind Junior. "So, your name is really Junior?" he slyly whispered.

"Of course not!" Junior laughed. "My real name—it's a secret. I'm like a 'junior' detective, so people began calling me Junior. It worked, so the name stuck."

Just when the crowd was starting to leave Junior's display, a sassy voice called out from the back of the group, "What the heck is going on here?"

The crowd split as a taller-than-average girl with long, pink hair came face-to-face with Silvis and Junior. She wore a pink hoodie and ripped jeans. "Detective services? You? You're just a kid. Like us," the girl challenged.

"I understand that it's hard to believe, but it's true. Hi," Junior extended his hand, "what's your name?"

"Elly," she snapped.

"Do you always split up the crowds?" Silvis teased.

"It's called popularity. It's my superpower," Elly bragged. "What's yours? Being a nobody?"

Silvis blushed, and before he could say anything, Elly kept talking. "Okay, Junior. I have a case to report. Do you think you can solve it?"

"I have an excellent track record," Junior replied enthusiastically, straightening his tie. "Please tell me about it."

Elly squinted. "How much will it cost me?"

"We can discuss payment after the case is solved."

Elly's face perked up. "I like the sound of that."

Junior smiled. "Good. Now tell me about your case, Elly."

"Okay. So, I met a kid a couple years older than us. His name was Zak. The Hawkman stole a necklace that my mom gave me, and I asked Zak to get it back. But then Zak disappeared. He hasn't been seen since. By anyone."

"When did this happen?" Junior scribbled in his notebook.

"About a week ago. My friend, Willow, says she knows something about the Hawkman, but I haven't seen her yet."

"I met Willow yesterday!" Silvis interrupted. Elly looked at Silvis like he was a dirty rag. Silvis added, "She said she worked for the Hawkman."

"Why would Willow be working with him and not tell me?" Elly mumbled in disbelief. "He's such a creepy guy."

Elly was interrupted as the school's staff yelled: "Recess is over! Get to your first class!"

Luckily, Junior was in Silvis's class, so he had a new friend. Willow was in their class, too. When she spotted Silvis, she glared and mouthed, "You little cheater!"

Silvis blushed. He had forgotten her ID card at home!

"Good morning, class. I'm Mrs. Coral. I will be your teacher this year. Let's start off by introducing ourselves to one another."

The introductions were very ordinary and dull until...

"H-hi. I'm Junior."

"Is Junior really your name?" someone called from the back of the room; there were some chuckles.

"Er... well, no, but that's what people call me."

The laughs returned when it came to Willow.

"I'm Willow."

"Like the trees?" someone said.

Willow turned around and glared at the bullies. "You're so typical, it's boring."

Eventually, the bells rang for afternoon recess. Silvis was quick to get to the playground; he wanted to find Elly to hear more about her missing friend, Zak.

"Hey! Wait up!" called Junior. "I never got your name, by the way."

"Silvis."

"Nice to meet you, Silvis. How long have you gone to school here?"

Before Silvis could tell the truth—that he hadn't gone here since kindergarten—his shoulder was yanked back.

"Where's my darn card, Silvis?!" Willow roared furiously. "I had to tell the school I forgot it so they would let me in."

"I don't have it right now. Sorry, Willow. But I can meet up at the park after school—a little later. Can I give you your card then? I left it at home."

"Fine."

With everything settled with Willow, Silvis and Junior saw Elly at the snack tables.

"Silvis, would you like to help me with this case?" Junior asked. "I could use an assistant."

"Yeah. I'd be glad to help," Silvis replied. "I don't have much detective experience, but I enjoy a good mystery." The two of them walked over to say hello to Elly.

"Hi, guys." Elly took a bite of her chocolate bar. She leaned forward and muttered, "I'm thinking of getting more help with the case—from a ... soldier I know."

Silvis and Junior exchanged glances. "Who is it?" they asked in unison.

"I'll tell you later. But take these for good luck." Elly handed two wild cards from a card deck to Silvis and Junior.

18

"Cool, thanks!" Junior said. And Silvis and Junior walked away and chatted with each other about their plans.

"Hey Silvis, after school we should circle up with Elly and meet at your house."

"Actually, I was gonna meet Willow after school, but you two can come, too. But let's not meet at my place; let's go to Newberry Park."

"Okay, got it," Junior said with a big smile.

•

When school ended, Silvis decided to walk home instead of ride the bus, so he had time to prepare for his meeting at Newberry Park. When he opened the door to his house. It was a wreck!

"Polo!" he screeched.

"Sorry," Polo replied. "Sometimes I just can't help it."

Silvis rolled his eyes. "Whatever! I'll clean this up later. I have to go."

"Where are you going?" Polo signed.

"Newberry Park."

"Can I please come with you?"

"No!"

"Please? I've been inside all day long."

Silvis gave in. He couldn't handle another mess. "Fine." Silvis knew he would have to reveal Polo to the others.

As they made their way to the park on Silvis's bicycle, Polo wouldn't stop nudging and hitting Silvis's back, which nearly made him crash—multiple times. There were many shouts of "Stop it!" and "Sorry!" and Polo needed to stop to pee—a lot. The ride should've taken about 30 minutes, but it took an hour.

Finally, Silvis reached Newberry Park, annoyed and relieved to be free of Polo's ape-ish needs, troubles, and tantrums. Silvis glanced at his watch: 5:46 p.m. He searched for a few minutes before he spied the group. They had all been waiting, so he decided to hide Polo behind him in hopes of it being a fun way to surprise them—to take the edge off him being late.

"There you are! Finally," Junior complained.

"So, guys—"

Without a warning, Polo peeked his head out from behind Silvis's back. Everyone screamed except Willow.

"What in God's name is an ape doing here?!" Elly shrieked.

"Gahhh!" Junior yelled.

"Relax! Relax, guys. He's my ape, and his name is Polo. He's super friendly. He's smart, too—he even knows sign language."

"What?" said Junior, suddenly intrigued.

Elly just shook her head and mumbled, "Ew."

"First things first, though." Willow wasn't going to let the meeting start without getting what she needed most. "Where's my card, Silvis?"

"I've got it right here." Silvis took the card out of his backpack and handed it to Willow.

"I was ready to turn you into a porkchop if you had forgotten it," Willow snarled.

Silvis ignored the odd comment.

"Okay, so ... did we just come all the way across town and wait an hour on Silvis only to talk about cards and apes? 'Cause if that's the case, I have better things to do." Elly crossed her arms.

"You're right, Elly. Let's get on about this case!" Junior said, winking at her.

Elly smiled smugly.

"What was your last conversation with Zak, Elly?" Junior asked while he opened his notebook.

"The last thing I remember was when he told me he had something to show me," said Elly.

"Okay. When was that? And did you ever see what he wanted to show you?"

"Two weeks ago. And no."

"Maybe what he wanted to show you had something related to his disappearance," Junior mused.

"But apparently he was spotted last week at the paintball field," said Elly.

Junior looked like he was about to say something, but he stopped himself.

"Junior, do you know something we don't?" Silvis pressed.

"Maybe," replied Junior. A white envelope slipped out of his backpack.

"What's in there?" Silvis asked.

"I—I'll show you tomorrow," Junior said, scrambling to put it away. "Elly—at recess you said you knew someone who could help us. Who is it?"

"He goes by 'Ghost.' I already had him looking into Zak's disappearance before I met you. I'm sure he can help us. He's the one who told me Zak was missing. I'll text his number to you."

"Thanks," said Junior. "Well, is that all, everyone?"

No one else had anything to say, so the friends said goodbye and each went their separate ways.

The next day at morning recess, Junior was acting weird. He was distracted and kept looking in the direction of the basketball courts. "What's going on?" Silvis finally asked.

"I texted Elly's friend Ghost yesterday and we agreed to meet up at the basketball courts," he mumbled to Silvis so no one would hear. "Want to come with me?"

Silvis nodded and followed Junior to the basketball courts.

Ghost looked very professional, wearing a suit and tie in a very formal manner, like Junior did. But Ghost didn't look like a detective; he looked like a secret agent of some sort.

"Hey, Silvis, this is Ghost," said Junior. "Ghost, this is Silvis. And I'm Junior."

"Hello, there," Ghost said. "Nice to meet you both. I'm here to help with the case of the missing boy."

"Are you sure this isn't some sort of prank or misunderstanding about Zak's disappearance?" said Junior.

"I'm certain it isn't," Ghost replied firmly. "He wouldn't disappear and not tell anyone."

"Interesting," said Junior. "Do you—"

But Ghost interrupted, "Sorry, I've gotta go. I'll talk to you later." And he jogged away.

That night, on his Segway, Junior drove through the streets. He heard shouts and yells in the distance. *What is going on?*

Whatever it was didn't matter right now. He had to see if the clue from the mysterious letter was true. Whoever had slipped the unsigned letter into his backpack told him that Zak was last spotted at the paintball field. Maybe there would be more clues there related to his disappearance.

Junior kept riding and thought about his older brother Bear, the house Bear made just for him, his Segway, his new friends, his great life—Bear had given him almost everything he could have wished for. But what was the most weird was that he never remembered Bear making the house or taking time off when they were homeless to build it. But he missed Bear's funny jokes, Bear's happy and cheerful mood, Bear's genius mind, and all the good he did for Junior. Junior was pretty sure Bear was dead, as no one had heard anything from him since he disappeared during his expedition two years ago. Dropping the sad topic, he continued riding until he arrived at the paintball field. It was deserted. As the clouds covered the evening sky, the field got creepy.

Still, Junior walked around the field. The only things he saw were leftover paintball guns and the arena stained with paintball marks. It seemed hopeless. *Zak couldn't be here.*

Crank!

Junior jumped and yelled. The noise came from a hut in the field.

As Junior approached the hut, he saw someone moving. A head peeked out of the hut, and then a person, a teen or adult, walked out. They were wearing paintball armor and a mask that looked like it was made of iron. The mask had two X's and a creepy smile on it. It looked like a dead person from cartoons.

"What's your name?" the person asked.

"J-Junior."

"Hello, Junior. I'm Ghast. Come on in."

Junior was terrified, but he did as the person ordered. He stepped inside, and then everything went black.

•

Junior woke up 20 minutes later. His head was bleeding, and his arms and legs had cuts all over them. He was inside the hut, but the person in the mask was nowhere to be seen. *I have to make a run for it,* he thought.

Junior immediately started running for his life. The person who had beat him up, Ghast, was probably some freak or psycho, but Junior couldn't be sure quite yet. *Zak was seen here,* he thought. *This guy could've been Zak himself.*

Junior was soon bleeding too much for his liking and was in too much pain to handle. Finally, he found his Segway and drove away with the last of his energy.

He didn't last very long. Two minutes later, once he was out of view of the field, he rolled off his Segway and lay wounded and in pain. He breathed heavily and tried to relax. Then he spied someone in the distance.

"H-help! H-help me! Please!" Junior called.

The figure approached him. Junior's mouth dropped open. It was Willow.

Willow helped Junior all the way to his house on foot, walking the Segway beside them. She helped clean some of his wounds.

"Now, explain!" Willow urged once Junior was cleaned up.

"Okay, okay," Junior said.

He pulled open all the drawers in his room until he found the note with the clues. "Someone gave me this. It's why I went to the paintball field," he said, handing her the letter to read:

Hello, Junior. I believe these details may help you with your case. Firstly, Elly is related to Zak, though she doesn't know it. Second, your new friend, Silvis, will be very helpful; he was doing something very suspicious last week the night Zak was last seen in the paintball field. I know you can solve this case. I gave you your clues. But beware . . be careful ... things may get dangerous.

At this point, Junior and Willow both wanted to drop the case. It was getting dangerous. But they knew they couldn't.

"If we solve it, we could get famous," Junior said.

"True," Willow agreed, "but is that worth dying for?"

Finally, Willow left, so Junior flicked on his favorite TV show, *The Investigation Feed,* and saw more about the murdered millionaire case he'd been following. And then he thought about his friends and the mystery. They were connected, for sure: Ghost, Elly, Willow, Silvis, and even himself. They were all connected. *Perhaps it is a setup,* he thought. *Perhaps someone intended to put the five of us together as a group to solve the mystery. Who would do that?*

And then the truth struck Junior: The one behind Zak's disappearance could be one of them. They would want to stay close to the investigation and pretend to be involved while really sending the group in the wrong directions. It had to be either Elly, Ghost, Silvis, or Willow.

There was a traitor among them. And a very smart one.

CHAPTER 3

PUZZLE

The next day on the morning news, Silvis saw videos and pictures of Griefings happening in their town. He'd never seen a Griefing before. In the videos, a group of people were causing annoyances and hurting everyone. Others were complaining that their possessions were missing. The griefers, small enough to be kids themselves, were running around in ski masks wreaking havoc on the town, particularly on Hillstretch Elementary. The whole neighborhood was filled with terror and screams.

Every channel had something about the Griefings. It was even on California Daily, one of the most famous news channels of California. And the weirdest part was that the Griefing only happened to Hillstretch Elementary and the kids who attended it.

After school that day, Silvis, Ghost, Junior, Elly, and Willow lay on the grass of Newberry Park. Ghost had informed them to wear their best clothes to the picnic he'd planned for this afternoon. Unlike her normal fashion, Willow was wearing a blue dress and skirt, which everyone agreed looked lovely. Elly didn't really care, and she wore what she always wore, a hoodie and ripped jeans. Ghost and Junior wore their normal formal suits and ties. Silvis wore some jeans and a coat and tie. He glanced at his bike, where he had left Polo. Polo seemed like he was behaving himself.

"I brought sandwiches," said Willow, holding up a plastic bag bulging with five sandwiches. "My mom made them."

"Great. We can eat those later. Let's discuss the case first," Junior said.

Silvis noticed that Junior had a large gash on his arm that wasn't there yesterday. He made a mental note to ask Junior about it later.

"Wait—what do you guys think about the Griefings?" Elly asked.

"The Griefings, yes, I think it might be connected to the case, but we know so little about it," said Junior.

"Why do you think it's connected to the case?" asked Ghost.

"The news said that they think the people causing the Griefings met up in a hut at the paintball field beforehand," said Junior. "I'll ... explain more about it later. Let's eat."

He's hiding something, thought Silvis. *I wonder what else he knows.* They finally ate Willow's mom's sandwiches.

"This sandwich is great," Silvis said, a mouth full of food.

"She's a great cook," Willow grinned.

"We're going to be late, guys. We should head back to the school now for that speech," Ghost said. Mr. Williams, the principal, had arranged a meeting that afternoon for all the students at Hillstretch Elementary—probably to calm everyone down about the Griefings.

What was Ghost's problem? Why is he always rushing away from things? Not that it's a bad thing, but it's weird, Silvis thought.

They packed up the food and picnic items and headed for their rides to the school. Elly's parents stopped at the park to drive her to the meeting. Willow, like she always did, walked instead of using a ride. Ghost screeched away on his motorcycle, which seemed smaller, like it was for teens. Junior hopped on his Segway. Silvis approached his bike, which Polo was messing around with.

"Ugh. You're always causing so much trouble!" Silvis yelled.

"I don't care," Polo replied, and he stuck out his tongue.

"You're going to that babysitter I hired for you. I spent half of my savings from the last six months on it."

"I'm not going to any babysitter!" Polo said, his hands moving quickly and menacingly.

Silvis sighed and got on his bike. He had to deal with another one of Polo's tantrums about going to the animal babysitter. Silvis ignored him for the rest of the ride. Fortunately, when they got to the animal babysitter, they had calmed him down using babysitter tricks.

Taking care of Polo made Silvis late again. Luckily, the meeting had only just started when he arrived. It was about the Griefings, as expected. Mr. Williams, the school principal, was hosting it and speaking to let people know more about it and how to help. Mr. Williams had clearly and strictly said that the meeting was only for students and parents weren't allowed to come.

The meeting was at Hillstretch Elementary's blacktop. There were hundreds of chairs set up for the kids to sit on. It was very surprising to Silvis, because he thought that, like any other meeting, the students had to sit on the ground of the blacktop.

Most of the school came for the meeting; only about 50 or less kids were missing. There were plenty of chairs left, and Silvis found a nice seat in the front row. Silvis spied Elly in the front row, as well as Ghost. After about five minutes, Mr. Williams must have felt like enough people had showed up, because he stood up and clapped his hands three times.

"Hello, students of Hillstretch!" Mr. Williams said with a very loud and clear voice, since there was no microphone. "As most of you know, this is about the Griefings. Most of them aren't crimes, but they are still very serious. And some, er, well, some *are* crimes. One of the worst crimes was Hillstretch students being drugged. A local teenager claimed he saw a man wearing a weird mask with X's on it giving them drugs that made them feel sleepy and weird. These students are now at the hospital. If you see someone with a mask that has X's on it, stay away from them and contact a parent or guardian."

The crowd mumbled in fear. Mr. Williams continued. "Many items from my office have been stolen, including my treasured trophies from my college football degree and my microphone. Students' school items, work, and treasured items have been stolen. There are also some weird kids who know kung fu and are beating people up. There are people Griefing, attacking, and committing crimes. We believe the griefers are students of Hillstretch, though their identities remain a mystery.

"Obviously, we need someone who can put an end to this. To stop it all. To get to the bottom of the mystery," said Mr. Williams. "Junior: please join me on the stage."

Junior looked like he was all nerves. He was nervous on the first day of school when a crowd of 30 people watched him. Now, there were hundreds of eyes locked on him. Junior's face turned red as he slowly walked up to the stage.

"H-hi," Junior stuttered, ripping the pipe that was smoking bubbles straight out of his mouth. He was already embarrassing himself.

"You sell yourself as a good detective, don't you?" prodded Mr. Williams.

"Yessir. I'm the best kid-detective, well, anywhere."

Mr. Williams chuckled along with the crowd. "So, do you want to solve this case? That's the impression our staff and students seem to have."
Junior chewed on his pipe. "Well, yes. But my work isn't free, Mr. Williams, much like your own work. Do you work for free?"

Mr. Williams smirked. "You can't be serious?"

Junior folded his arms. "If you go without pay for being our principal, I'll go without pay to find out who's behind these Griefings."

Mr. Williams pulled out his wallet and handed Junior a $50 bill. "Is this a good start?"

"Let's solve this case!" Junior said, swiping the money from Mr. Williams's hand.

About five seconds later, a bunch of $10 bills flew from the audience straight at Junior. Now, they had probably given him around $200 in total, and he seemed a hundred percent satisfied.

Mr. Williams smiled. "Does anyone have any questions?" he asked. The crowd was silent. "Alright, then, well, thank you, Junior! That concludes the meeting."

The staff began moving the chairs and disassembling the stage as the kids left.

"Silvis," Junior began. "I have something to tell you. Needs to be private. Come over to my house after the meeting. And thank you for the money."

"No problem," Silvis winked.

Junior rode his Segway and Silvis rode his bike. They rode for an hour instead of the normal 15 minutes because the tourism was high and people wanted to see the scene and the Griefing details. The town was a mess. There was garbage all over the streets, shattered windows, trampled flowerbeds, and random household objects scattered around.

Finally, they arrived. Silvis's bike screeched into the driveway. He hopped off it and pulled the bike stand up.

They walked inside Junior's laboratory-like house. Silvis didn't give any compliments because he was feeling uneasy, and he was pretty sure whatever Junior wanted to tell him wasn't going to be good, considering Junior brought him all the way into his house. Junior began hunting through his shelves and cabinets, ramming them open like a wild animal that had no care about its surroundings.

"Uhh, Junior, what are you doing?" Silvis was feeling even more nervous, and his face began to turn red.

"Hold on a sec," Junior replied. Finally, he fished a piece of paper out of a closet. "At last!"

"What is that?"

Junior unfolded the paper to reveal the letter that had fallen out of his backpack at their first meeting at the park. "Look," Junior began. "I'm sorry I kept it a secret, but with all the Griefings, I had to show you. But don't tell anyone else, especially not Elly."

Silvis snatched the piece of paper out of Junior's hands and raised an eyebrow. He was shocked to see these weird clues. *Elly's related to Zak? I was doing something suspicious the night Zak was last seen?*

Junior told him all about when he was attacked by Ghast at the paintball field. "So that's why you have all those scratches!" said Silvis.
Silvis wasn't really mad about Junior keeping it all a secret, considering that if it were his decision, he probably would've done the same thing.

"If Elly was related to Zak, she very much could've well, er, y'know, done something bad to him and made him disappear, then hired you just to put you off track on the case. Maybe she's causing all the Griefings," Silvis suggested.

"That could be true. But we can't just say that without proof. We need to find out more until we can be assured that a possibility or theory is definitely true," stated Junior.

Silvis rolled his eyes. "You're right."

"Also, can we call Ghost? I think he can help us," said Junior.

"Sure thing. But I don't have a good feeling about him. He's very shady and mysterious," said Silvis.

Twenty minutes later, the doorbell at Junior's house rang. "I'll get the door," Silvis said.

Silvis opened the door and Ghost walked in. He was dressed casual, in a white T-shirt, black vest, and jeans, instead of in his normal suit.

"Hello, Silvis!" Ghost said.

"Hi, Ghost. We were trying to solve our case and we wanted some of your help."

"Sure. I'll definitely help."

The three of them got adjusted and Junior even poured them cups of hot tea. That was when Junior explained to them his theory: "I think this is all a setup. All these Hillstretch kids coming together plotting something, Griefing the school ... someone must be behind it all. The ultimate plot, organized by a mastermind. It's like chess. The griefers are the pawns and the mastermind is the queen. It's our job to knock out the pawns, but in the end, taking them all out will be too much of a sacrifice. But if we make the queen checkmate, then we win. And one more thing. I think that someone in our group is a traitor. I feel like someone is spying on us."

"That's a very interesting theory. It might be true," said Silvis. "But who is the king or queen behind this all? And how can we trap them?"

"Good question," Ghost said. "Also, we know that the pawns are the griefers, but who are the rooks, bishops, and knights?"

"Very interesting," Junior noted. "We don't know. Hey, Ghost, do you play chess?"

"I sure do. I love the game; it's my most favorite. People say I'm a grand master."

"Do you wanna play a game?"

"Er, I have to get going soon."

"Please, Ghost, just one game."

"Okay, fine. I will."

As the two of them grabbed the chess board and set up the game, Silvis said, "I think your theory that one of us is a traitor is interesting, but I really feel like all of us are innocent. Maybe it's all a misunderstanding and someone random that knows we're investigating this case is spying on us and gaining information." Junior ignored him. He was way too busy doing his opening on the chess board and thinking hard about what move Ghost would make.

Silvis was quite bored. Ghost and Junior were playing chess, and obviously, two chess champions like them could have a game that went on forever. Silvis roamed around Junior's house whistling a lullaby that his mom, whom he barely could remember, used to sing to him. He was hoping to find a secret or another clue that Junior had possibly hid from him as well.

After a while, Silvis had found nothing. He was pretty sure Junior had told him all the secrets. Junior's house was pretty big. Silvis was surprised that Junior lived in such a big house alone and wondered who had made it. The walls of Junior's house were painted with smooth and shiny gray paint. His floors were mostly made from white colored marble, except for the carpeted parts. He had a big dining table to eat his meals on, which looked like it could fit a whole family of eight or more people. But clearly, the huge table was only used by a skinny eleven-year-old boy. *Did he ever live with someone else? Is that why his house is so big and can hold that many people?* Silvis thought.

Silvis thought he had finally seen everything in Junior's lab-like house. But then he bumped into a plain wall when he wasn't looking. It turned out to be an door, not a wall. The door slid open, revealing what could have only been an elevator. Silvis stumbled into the elevator, still holding his now-swollen head in pain.

"What is this?" Silvis said. "I knew it! Junior did have more secrets."

Silvis spied a button in the corner of the elevator. There weren't multiple levels; instead, there was only one level you could go to, and that level was the basement.

"Junior has a basement?" Silvis knew he was onto something. Junior was very mysterious, and Silvis knew it from the start. He pressed the button and the elevator began to descend.

When door finally fully opened. Silvis ran through it immediately. His mouth dropped open. It looked like a laboratory.

But it wasn't just a laboratory. It was filled with banners about mystery shows and real-life cases hanging on the white walls; there were beautiful paintings hung up, different items packed in boxes like they were in storage, Junior's awards and detective achievements, and, what caught Silvis the most by surprise, pictures of Junior's family with Junior as a baby and child. Whatever was in the boxes and the other things in the lab, Silvis didn't look at, because he didn't want to look through Junior's personal stuff.

Junior does have a secret. But there's nothing to do with the case down here. Or at least I don't think so. I should probably get back upstairs before they start wondering where I went. Silvis skipped over to the elevator. He felt like he had gotten a gold medal, and he was so cheerful and bright because he got to know Junior more by coming down here.

Silvis sat down on the floor of the elevator. He thought about the case and what they knew: Zak's disappearance and the Griefings were probably connected, and one of his friends might be a traitor. Of course, he had probably thought about the clues a million times and gotten no good answer, but he was determined to solve the case. It was his destiny to crack it. *Not my destiny. It's Junior's. It's his case anyways,* Silvis thought to himself.

He was getting frustrated about how poor their progress was. *Zak was seen in the paintball field. Junior went there and was assaulted by some guy who probably has mental issues. This guy would have definitely done something to Zak. But by the way Junior described him, he was definitely a teen or adult,* Silvis thought. *And I was doing something suspicious the night he was seen? Elly is related to Zak and doesn't know it?*

That's when it hit Silvis. He didn't know which day Zak was seen in the paintball field and who saw him, but the only day Silvis ever did something that was sort of suspicious was the day he and Polo went to the Hawkman's house for Willow's card. Silvis and Polo's plan had been to steal the card, and that was pretty suspicious.

But Willow ended up giving us her card. That's not suspicious, he thought to himself. *It must've been my surroundings that were. Is Willow the one that the clue was pointing out? Or the house? The most likely answer is, of course, the Hawkman. He is super shady. This has something to do with him.*

Silvis's frown turned to a smile and then a chuckle. "I did it! I found a big piece. Without Junior's help!" Silvis thought about what Junior had found so far. As far as he knew, it was barely anything. The clues Junior had were just the ones the unknown source had given, not his own discoveries. Silvis felt proud of himself.

Lost in his thoughts, Silvis didn't realize that the elevator door had begun to open. It was the slow creak that made the hairs on his neck stand up. At first, he sprang to his feet, whipping his tie straight out of his suit like a mental patient. He held the tie out, ready to whip an intruder in the face, when he realized his stupidity again.

"The elevator strikes again," Silvis muttered. He heard laughs and chattering coming from Junior's table. He approached the noise and saw Junior and Ghost laughing their heads off. The chess board was tipped upside down and chess pieces were scattered across the room.

"What the—"

Junior and Ghost turned to Silvis, still laughing.

Silvis opened his mouth to speak, but Junior cut him off. "It was a tie. We calculated everything. It was a tie. None of us had a way to checkmate. I was winning for the first half. Then Ghost picked up his game and took my queen, only to fall into my trap! And I took his queen, as well as his last knight. It was a queen-for-queen sacrifice, but I was on the upper hand 'cause I got his horse as well. Then, he cornered my king with an army of pawns, but he didn't see my bishop's free opening. I killed all his pawns with my bishop and a pawn."

"I should've checkmated you there for sure. You're lucky you pulled off the bishop tactic," said Ghost.

"And the flipped board and scattered pieces?" Silvis asked.

"Oh, he got mad I escaped the checkmate and flipped over the board after we tied," said Ghost.

"Silvis ... you look like you know something we don't. Like you learned it just now," said Junior.

"What are you talking about?" said Silvis.

"Yeah," Ghost tuned in. "Where were you all this time?"

"Uhh ... okay, maybe I do know something."

"So," Ghost said, shooting a glare at Silvis. "What did you find out?"

Silvis explained to them his theory.

"You're a genius!" said Junior.

"You're smarter than the detective!" blurted Ghost.

At first, a smile spread across Silvis's face, and he felt like his bucket was filled up.

Junior offered coffee, but he fixed them some warm hot chocolate instead because Ghost insisted he didn't want to be awake all night. Junior also gave them some cookies and cupcakes. As Silvis bit into the cupcake, he tasted the creamy vanilla frosting melt in his mouth as he closed his eyes and imagined he was bathing in cupcakes, all of different flavors but all delicious.

"Mmm," Silvis said, with a mouthful of frosting. He was too busy imagining he was in a plane made of cupcakes in his cupcake world that he didn't realize both Junior and Ghost were tugging on his shoulder.

"It was just a mystery and now it's a whole puzzle to solve. We gotta find the pieces and put them together to solve the case, as well as beat our enemy in a game of chess," Junior said. "We have made some progress."

"But the very likely idea that one of us in this very room could be a dangerous criminal and the one behind it all is scary," Silvis said, gazing at the chess pieces all over the floor with a worried frown. *What if one of us is a criminal? What if this person is targeting us?* Silvis frowned.

"Well, uh, it was a pleasure to be with you boys, but I've really got to go," Ghost interrupted. He got up from the ground, stepped over the chess pieces, picked up his bag, and headed for the door.

"Not so fast!" Junior screeched.

"W-what?" Ghost asked with a very agitated voice. He rolled up his sleeve and looked at the time. "I, er—"

"No!" Junior roared. "You're forgetting the mess you made! Help me clean it up." Junior pointed his skinny bony finger at the scattered chess pieces.

"Ugh, alright," said Ghost.

"And you too, Silvis!" Junior added as Silvis began going for the door.

"What? Me? You guys made this mess, so I shouldn't need to clean up anything," said Silvis.

"I don't care," Junior said with a deep and tired voice.

He must be stressed out with everything, Silvis thought. "Fine." He rolled his eyes.

They began picking up pieces. With the three of them cleaning, they finished collecting the little chess pieces after only three minutes. They were all happy to finish so fast, since the chess pieces were hidden across the room and some even outside.

Ghost sighed, said goodbye, and then walked out, slamming the door shut. They heard an eerie screech and then a vroom. They shut their ears tight until the noise faded. Junior rolled his eyes. "That stupid motorcycle is way too loud." Junior needed to buy some supplies for the store, so Silvis stayed around and watched TV while he was gone.

An hour later, Junior returned. "Stay over for the night, would ya?"

"But Polo—"

"Don't mind Polo. I've got him working on something."

"What! You saw Polo and assigned him to a job?" Silvis was far too confused.

"He's doing some hacking for me," Junior said with a proud grin. "When it comes down to it, I find a way to get the job done. I found the ol' ape being chased by an old lady. I took him in and told the lady I'd take care of him. He's in the attic room. I'm pretty sure he's napping."

Silvis frowned. "Hacking is one of Polo's bad skills."

"But it's helping us solve the case. Thank God almost everyone on Newburg Street knows sign language."

"Wow, even the babysitter failed. But how were you able to take care of him?" Silvis asked.

"I dunno. Wanna see him?"

"Sure."

They walked up the smooth marble stairs of Junior's house. It was basically a mansion. Silvis creeped cautiously and walked slowly and as silent as an ant.

"What are you doing?!" Junior blurted.

"Shhh!" Silvis whispered. "We can't wake up that ape. He'll cause havoc!"

Silvis told Junior with his sharp blue eyes staring into Junior's brown eyes. "No, it's fine. I got him under control. Better than that babysitter. He will listen now."

Silvis couldn't believe it. How could a kid, just like Silvis and his same age, be able to control a whiny ape better than a babysitter that cost $200? He knew he would demand a refund the next day.

Junior, standing on his very tippy toes, reached for a shiny dangling rod that looked like one of the switches at Silvis's house that activated his fan. He almost fell, unable to grasp it.

"Need a hand?" Silvis asked him, staring at Junior and making him look stupid.

"Duh." Junior rolled his eyes.

Silvis faked a cough to release the giggle was holding in.

Junior sighed. "You're only three inches taller than me. There's no reason to laugh."

Silvis's face turned red. "I, er—"

Junior narrowed his eyes and gave him a "don't argue" look. Silvis stepped forward and reached for the rod. Even though he had to go on his tippy toes, he got the rod. He couldn't manage a slow pull, so he yanked at the rod and a folded ladder came falling down, just missing his head. "Something isn't right with this stupid stuff. I'm always getting jump-scared."

Junior and Silvis climbed up the ladder, careful not to fall. They creeped into the dark attic, but with Junior at his side, Silvis didn't feel very frightened by the silent darkness. Junior was experienced and wasn't really scared of anything (except for a creepy guy wearing a mask with X's on it).

At first, Silvis was sure there was no chance anyone was here and Polo must've been possessed by a ghost. As they crawled further into the dark abyss of the attic, they both heard music in the distance and soon caught a glimpse of light.

"That's him?" Silvis asked.

"What is he doing?! I thought he was sleeping!" Junior said quietly.

They finally made it to the light, where they saw Polo eating chips and two empty soda cans lying on a red blanket underneath him. Polo had a headset on, and it was plugged into a speaker right next to him. Polo was dancing like a monkey would.

"Polo!" Silvis bellowed. He yanked the plug of Polo's headset straight out of the speaker to reveal a rap song, swear words spewing out of the radio.

"What is this?" Silvis yelled, still disturbed by all the swears coming from the rap song. "What the heck are you listening to?! You're just a young ape!" He immediately muted the volume of the speaker.

Polo wore a guilty look on his face, full of sorrow.

Silvis asked, "Where did you get those headphones?"

"I found these weird things and that speaker in the babysitter's backpack. I clicked a button that said 'My Playlist' on this phone," Polo said in sign language, like always.

"You stole her phone too!"

"Well, now I'm vibin' to this epic music," Polo said. "Until you had to ruin it!" He frowned.

Silvis opened his mouth, but then Junior, who was staring at a wall, erupted in laughter. "Hahahaha!" he thundered. He couldn't stop laughing, like the first day of school when Silvis asked him if Junior was really his name.

"What is so damn funny?" Silvis yelled. His face was already red enough after hearing the songs that Polo was listening to.

"Th-the—"

"The what?" Silvis sputtered. He could tell Junior was laughing so hard he couldn't say the proper words.

"The b-babysitter. That's what she listens to!" Junior exclaimed, still laughing.

"That's right! She listens to that song full of swears. She seemed so innocent ..." Silvis also began bursting with laughter. Polo, who didn't really understand what was funny, began laughing too.

Silvis composed himself. "You and me are gonna have a talk at home," he told Polo sternly.

"You and I," Junior corrected.

Silvis rolled his eyes. "Whatever."

"What are we gonna do with him?" Junior asked.

"Keep him here in the attic for the night, I guess."

"Are you sure that's a good idea? He's not gonna mess around again?"

"Today's been a stressful and tiring day. I really don't wanna spend more time babysitting him."

Polo scowled and hopped away very slyly.

"Ughh!" Silvis began. "Not again! He ran away again. I should've gotten a dog instead of him. But I had to take that naughty ape."

"How did you get him?" Junior asked.

"Well, it's a complicated story, but basically, he was a baby when I found him, and his mother had something to do with my parents, so she left Polo at my house a day after—" He closed his mouth, unable to finish.

"After what?"

"Never mind."

Unlike many others, Junior respected Silvis's privacy and didn't insist on knowing.

"I'll fix us a good dinner," Junior said, walking to the kitchen. Junior had an oven, and he cooked some bread that had a delicious and rich smell. Silvis's mouth watered.

"So, how do you make your food?" Junior asked Silvis.

"I don't make it."

"Then who does?"

Silvis pointed upstairs. "The ape."

"Polo can cook?!" Junior blurted, as his oven mitts fell right off his hands.

"I told you, he's a skilled and naughty little ape."

"But I didn't know he was that smart," Junior said in disbelief.

The oven stopped making a tik-tik-tik noise. Junior, who had forgotten to put his oven mitts back on, quickly scavenged the floor, and, like an eagle, he swooped to his prey (the oven mitts). He slipped on the wet floor and almost tripped.

All of this drama was lovely, entertaining, and hilarious for Silvis. He watched as Junior struggled back to his feet. Silvis hid a smile and snicker.

Once again, Silvis got a good whiff of the delicious smell. Junior grabbed the bread and cut it into pieces for the two of them, saving a bit for Polo. "Enjoy!" Junior said, munching into the bread.

The two boys munched and savored the flavorful delicious bread until they were too full have another bite.

"Enjoyed it?" Junior asked.

A big grin spread across Silvis's face. "You already know my answer."

Junior beamed, too. "I'm sorry about dinner being so late, but we should sleep now. It's 11:30."

"Alright," Silvis replied.

They washed their hands and took a sip of their ice-cold sodas and headed upstairs for bed.

Junior led Silvis to a room with a bunk bed. "I sleep here every night. I wish Bear was here to sleep with me," Junior said to him.

"Who's Bear?"

"My brother. He ... passed away."

"I'm sorry," said Silvis.

"It's okay. It's been a long time."

They huddled into the beds after a long argument over who got the top bunk (Silvis won).

CHAPTER 4
SECRET KEY

The winds were heavy as the sun had almost sunk almost out of sight and the night began to creep into the skies of Hillstretch city. Silvis biked home to his with Polo on his back and breaked at a stop sign.

"Why'd you stop!" Polo signaled.

"Ugh, don't you know anything about street rules?"

"Streets have rules?"

Silvis rolled his eyes. He was tired of hearing his stupid questions; he needed to teach Polo some sense.

Silvis continued on his bike and he saw the Community House ahead. "Look! It's the new Community House!" exclaimed Polo.

"You've never seen the new Community House before?" Silvis said in surprise.

"Nope."

Right as they reached the Community House, Silvis stopped to admire the place, which looked like a school on the outside but not on the inside. The Community House was now closed. Silvis watched Polo gaze at it and chuckled. Silvis was about to leave when he heard a faint noise coming from the Community House.

Silvis parked his bike behind a tall nearby bush so no one would know that he was on the Community House's grounds at night.

"What are you doing?!" said Polo.

"Am I hearing something, or did you hear that noise too?"

"I did," replied Polo.

"Okay, well, I think we should investigate," Silvis said.

Polo nodded.

Silvis crept forward, Polo still on his back, and moved towards the noise. As they moved, the noise got louder and louder, and then they got to the Community House door. It was, of course, locked, but now Silvis could hear the noise louder and clearer. It sounded like ... music. Ballet music. Silvis leaned his head onto the door to hear better as Polo watched. The door sprang open.

No one was on the other side.

"Wait, no one is here," Silvis began. "That means ... the door was unlocked!"

Polo gasped. "Uh oh ..."

Silvis sneaked into the Community House and walked around, following the music. It was dark inside, but not too creepy. For some reason, the janitor's things were left behind in the entrance. There were papers scattered all over the ground, messy desks, and old furniture. Silvis was no detective, but he could tell something had happened here.

Silvis continued along, going closer towards the music. It seemed like the janitor had cleaned everything up since the last visit here, but why did he leave his tools behind?

Just then, Silvis realized that the music was coming from under him. "Oh yeah, the Community House has a basement with a stage," Silvis whispered to Polo.

"I don't like basements," Polo said. "They creep me out."

"Me too." Silvis felt like going back to the bike and biking home. This could be a bad idea and something bad might happen, like how Junior got attacked by Ghast. "I know it's creepy, Polo, but I have to get to the bottom of this. I'm too curious," Silvis told him sternly.

"Okay," Polo replied, frowning.

Silvis opened the basement door, which he spied nearby. He descended some stairs, and then he heard the music extremely clear, as if he and Polo were only a few feet away from it.

Sure enough, they were. There was a large stage, and it had a few spotlights to show 10 girls, probably about seven years old, doing ballet.

The theater seats were completely empty, except for one person. Silvis could only see the back of their head. They were female and they had long blond hair. "Great job, girls! We're gonna win the top prize, for sure!" the girl in the audience said.

"That's Elly!" Silvis whispered. "I recognize her voice."

"What is she doing here?" Polo asked.

"I have no idea," Silvis said in sign language to be as quiet as possible. Elly was telling the girls to move a bit, fix their stances, training them as they did the ballet, as classical music blared through the room. Silvis couldn't make out how Elly got in the Community House or why she chose to come here when it had closed a few hours ago. But clearly, she was coaching these girls in ballet.

"Good job, girls!" Elly called out. "Now, let's all take a break."

Some of the dancers said "yes" and some nodded their heads. The girls left the room, leaving Silvis and Polo alone.

"Why are they here after the Community House is closed?" asked Polo.

Silvis shrugged. "Let's keep looking around."

"Wait!" said Polo, pointing to the theater seats. There was a janitor's cart in one of the aisles.

"Uh, that wasn't here when we got here ..." said Polo.

Silvis's eyebrows cocked up. "I know," he said. "Someone was here, and we didn't even see them."

Polo scavenged the janitor's supplies: a trash bin, mops, water, and disinfecting sprays.

"Oooo," Polo said with his speaking voice. "Something shiny!"

Something golden shone in the janitor's cart. Polo grabbed it without a single sign of hesitation, full of excitement.

"A key!" Silvis gasped.

"Yes, yes, very shiny," Polo said.

"Maybe the person who was here left the key here on purpose so someone could use it ... or maybe not," said Silvis.

"Smart thinking," Polo replied. "Now, let's search for whatever that key unlocks."

They searched the room and brought the janitor's supplies and cart with them backstage.

"Looook," Polo said in his own voice again.

Silvis was observing a disinfectant spray. He whipped around, surprised that Polo said a word aloud again. Polo was pointing to a curtain.

"Polo! Don't waste my time! It's not funny!"

"No, no, look closer!"

Silvis studied the curtain and saw something in the corner of the curtain. It looked like the corner of a door! "Polo! Great find!" he cheered, and they hurried over the curtain.

Silvis pulled the curtain to reveal a dark blue door with a keyhole in the doorknob.

"Try the key here!" said Silvis.

Polo put the key in the hole. "It doesn't work," Polo said.

"No, silly, turn the key counter-clockwise," said Silvis.

"What's that mean?"

"Ugh, just turn it to the left."

Polo turned the key and Silvis pushed the door open. Inside was a bunker that had Nerf guns, paintball, airsoft vests, and helium.

"Wow," said Polo. As they were admiring it, sounds of footsteps and muttering voices came from outside the basement.

"Someone's here!" Silvis gasped. He pushed the janitor cart inside the room and pulled Polo in the room with him.

"The curtain," Polo said.

Silvis quickly opened the door. "The key! Gimme it!" Silvis snarled.

"But—"

Silvis snatched the key from Polo, shoved it into the keyhole, and turned it. Then he placed it in his pocket, where it could be safe.

"Now we're safe," he whispered. "It's probably just a security guard. But what if they attack us? I definitely don't wanna die young."

Polo snickered. "You're gonna die and so am I. It's not fair. You get a longer life than me anyways."

"You get 40 years! Unless we die now. Don't complain unless you wanna live when I'm an old man with a cane."

Polo chuckled and hopped away.

The voices outside were slightly louder. Silvis sat down on a bench in the room and sighed. The entire room had beautiful quartz floors and walls. There were paintball guns everywhere. Silvis had a few airsoft guns in his basement, but they were nowhere near as good as the ones in the room.

"Polo," said Silvis.

There was no response.

"Polo!"

Nothing.

"I need your help, Polo."

Silvis looked behind him. Polo was standing there in armor, holding an airsoft sniper. He had two swords sheathed behind his back.

"Polo, I—"

Polo pulled out a sword and put it to Silvis's neck. The sword was shining bright blue and it looked very sharp. Silvis gulped hard. Was this it? Was he about to get killed by an angry ape? Would he be able to say any last words? Polo lowered the sword. He howled in laughter. "You really thought I'd kill you!"

Silvis's face turned pink. *I'm such a fool! Why would I think Polo would kill me?!*

"So, what do you need?" asked Polo.

"Uh, I don't know what to do here. When should we leave?"

"Well, why are you asking me these questions, do I look like Sherlock Holmes?!" Polo said.

"Oh, you lazy little ape," said Silvis. "Let's wait here until we're sure that the people outside are gone."

•

Thirty minutes later, Polo's thunderous snores of doom woke Silvis. Silvis's shirt was on his chin, he was leaning on a wall, and his belly was exposed. He was still half asleep, but then Polo's snores intensified.

"Ah!" Silvis shouted. A drop of saliva dripped on Silvis's shirt. When he realized he was drooling, he wanted to scream, laugh, and cry all at the same time, but he couldn't choose one, so he kept quiet and wiped his drool away. He gave his shirt a disgusted look and then shifted it, but it wouldn't go straight. So he got up and then put it on properly.

Meanwhile, Polo's snores were too loud and torturous to handle. Silvis followed the snores until he thought he felt his ears burst. He found Polo sleeping on the floor with an airsoft gun on his belly, his swords all over the floor.

"Polo!"

He did not stir.

Silvis walked over to Polo, kneeled, and shook Polo seventeen times.

"Blakagargh?" Polo said with his mouth.

"Having a weird dream?" Silvis asked him.

Polo shook himself to normal. "Yeah," he signed.

"I think it's about time we get outta here," Silvis said. "I don't hear anything. Polo, c'mon."

Polo hopped onto Silvis's back, and without stalling, Silvis opened the door. No one was backstage. The janitor's cart was gone.

"Well, it's good to know they're not camping us, but they may still be here somewhere," Silvis remarked. "And it looks like they put the cart back where it belongs."

Still cautious, Silvis tiptoed, determined not to make a sound. They exited the backstage area, ready to run if someone came. They stopped for a moment, studying the big stage that barely had any lighting. They didn't hear anyone.

They ventured onward, keeping a high look out. Silvis had his eyes narrowed, ready to find a trap or security guard, and Polo had his eyes wide open. Silvis stuffed his hand in his pocket to make sure the key was there. It was there, with a satisfying cold feeling.

They made it to the Community House main entrance, the same one he and Polo went through earlier. He placed his hand on the doorknob and twisted it open.

There was only one thing out of the ordinary outside the Community House: a black SUV parked on the other side of the road, empty and turned off.

Silvis walked towards his bike, which he had only seen because a tiny bit of one of the big black wheels stuck out from this angle. "Alright, Polo, let's go home. Tonight has been super crazy, like a little too adventurous."

"I won't forget punching those girls!" Polo said.

Silvis stepped onto the bike. The moment he started cycling, the black SUV's engine revved. Silvis stared at it, puzzled.

It charged towards him. "AHHHH!" Silvis screamed. He cycled as fast as he could. "Polo, look back and tell me who's in that car! Also, put your hands in front of my face so I can see what you're saying."

There was no immediate answer, but it was probably because Polo was freaking out. After a few seconds, Polo stuck his hands in front of Silvis's face and said, "They're getting closer, so we gotta hurry! The driver is a man. I can't make out who he is, though, it's too dark."

Silvis nodded and kept pedaling. The car was close. *Is this really the end?* Silvis thought. He knew he couldn't outrun the car for long, and it seemed impossible for them to escape it. But Silvis fought off the negative thoughts and replaced them with positive ones. *You've survived so much, how could you die now?*

Silvis began losing his grip on the bike. The bike went charging towards a tree. Oh, boy!" Silvis said. Right before he hit the tree, he jumped off the bike and grabbed Polo's hand. They tumbled through the grass and slammed into a fence.

Silvis's vision was blurry. He tried getting up, but he couldn't. His head and right leg were too weak after the crash. Polo howled in pain.

Silvis thought about the people that he loved, but he realized the only family he could remember was Polo. He peered up at the moon. That would be the last thing he saw before he died, before he became a nobody. *But I'm already just a stupid nobody. Nobody knew who I was for years and years,* he thought.

Silvis sighed and closed his eyes. Any moment now, the SUV would reach him and run him over. This was it ...

Screeeech! Silvis jolted upright. The SUV had crashed into a fence in front of a house. Polo was knocked out cold. Silvis picked him up.

Vrooom! A black miniature motorcycle stopped next to Silvis. "Huh?" Silvis said.

A boy stepped off of the miniature motorcycle and took off his helmet.

"Ghost?!" Silvis gasped.

"Someone had to save your butts," said Ghost, helping Silvis up and giving him a clap on the shoulder.

"But—"

"No time; we have to get out of here. That SUV is crazy!" Ghost gestured for Silvis to get on the motorcycle.

Silvis had so many questions, but his main priority was to escape. He stepped onto the backseat of the motorcycle, clutching Polo.

"Wait!" said Silvis before Ghost could start the motorcycle. He stuffed his hand into his pocket. Silvis gasped.

"Oh no! How!" Silvis asked.

"What's the matter?" Ghost asked.

"The key! It's gone!"

"What key? You're being super suspicious. I don't even know what you're doing here, being chased by an SUV." Ghost started the motorcycle before Silvis could reply, and then they zoomed away.

I can't believe I lost the key!

"So, what key are you talking about?" Ghost asked.

"In the Community House basement, we found—"

"What on earth were you doing there? It's been closed for almost two hours now!"

Silvis sighed. "I'll explain the whole story. You don't have to believe me." He told Ghost about the bunker they'd found, and the strange janitor's cart.

"How did you find me here?" asked Silvis.

"My granny told me to pick up some medicine from the local pharmacy for her and she gave me a few dollars." Ghost showed Silvis the money. "So then, on my way, I saw an SUV chasing you, so I threw a ninja star at it and it crashed." Ghost held up a shiny metal ninja star.

"So, *you* made the car crash," Silvis said. "And that thing looks epic. I underestimated your power."

"Well, everyone does," Ghost replied. "We're almost at your house."

"My bike! I left it by the Community House," said Silvis.

"Don't worry, I'll bring it back for you," said Ghost. "I have to go to my violin lesson first, though."

"You play the violin?" said Silvis. "Me too."

"Cool," said Ghost. "Here we are. Go take care of that ape."

•

Once they were home, in his bunker basement, Silvis searched Polo's body for any wounds. Polo whined at Silvis's touch. There was a scrape on the back of Polo's head, and it had a swollen bump. "Stay here, I'll get the alcohol swabs."

Silvis came back with alcohol swabs and Polo howled in fear. It wasn't the first time he got alcohol swabs; he had gotten them many times from wounds or scratches, and they stung a lot. Silvis dabbed Polo's wound and Polo screamed in pain.

"It's okay, bud," Silvis told him. He put a cotton swab on Polo's wound and then put medical tape on the swab. "You should be fine in a few days."

"Such a crazy day," said Polo.

"We should get some rest."

Polo nodded his head lightly, careful not to hurt himself. Silvis put Polo in his bright blue cradle that glowed at night. Polo loved it and slept in it every night. He'd had it as long as Silvis could remember.

After seven minutes, Silvis heard Polo's snores. Then someone rang the doorbell. It was Ghost, returning his bike. Ghost was in a big hurry to leave, though, so they barely even talked.

Silvis tiptoed to the printer in the basement. There was so much junk, and Silvis had no plans on cleaning any of it tonight.

Silvis snatched a piece of high-quality paper from the printer. He thought of the lost key for a second, then stopped. *The key doesn't have any use to me, so why am I thinking about it?* His eyes found something else on the table. A playing card. It was the wild card Elly had given him on the first day of school.

Me, Elly, Junior, Ghost, and Willow. They must've all been Junior's prime suspects, except himself, Silvis thought. *And the pawns, they could be anyone. They're like ... like wild cards.*

"Tomorrow, we will have a meeting," Silvis wrote. "We will make a new plan to catch the pawns." But he couldn't stop thinking about how the pawns were like wild cards. So he crossed it out and wrote something new: "Tomorrow, we will have a meeting. We will make a new plan to catch the wild cards."

CHAPTER 5
PAWN HUNT

Silvis gasped and woke up from a terrifying dream. He coughed for a second. He had fallen asleep while waiting for Junior, Elly, Ghost, and Willow at Newberry Park.

"Ugh, lazy bum," a voice said.

Junior, Elly, Ghost, and Willow were directly above him, staring at him, and Elly had just called him a lazy bum.

His cheeks turned red. "Well—"

"No," Elly said. "Tell us why you called us here. That creepy ape better not be here."

Elly had no patience for anything. At this point, Silvis began to doubt whether Elly even cared about Zak's case.

"Okay, okay," Silvis began. "The ape is hurt, so he's not here."

"And why were you gasping and choking?" Willow chuckled.

"Just a bad dream," Silvis mumbled.

"You were *dreaming* while we searched for you! What an idiot," Elly jeered.

Silvis's cheeks turned red again. He felt like a reject. *It's because I've lived alone and have barely gone outside,* Silvis thought to himself to make him feel better. But something inside him told him that wasn't true, that he really was a reject, and it drained his positivity. Silvis didn't know how to reply to Elly.

For a moment, none of them spoke. The park was peaceful and birds chirped while other kids' laughs echoed across the grass. Silvis felt like nature was his only friend. Nature was the only thing that made him feel better and brought positivity to him.

As he was deep in his thoughts, Ghost interrupted and said, "God, spill the beans! I don't got all day. There's places I need to be!"

"I'm sorry," Silvis replied. "But we need a solid plan. This case is becoming dangerous."

"That's exactly why we should quit," Willow said.

He could understand why she thought this way, because of Ghast attacking Junior.

"Well, we can't quit," said Silvis.

"That's right," Junior said.

Willow gave him an "are you crazy?!" look, but he didn't seem to notice.

"Silvis, Ghost, and I made a way to display this using a chessboard. The pawns would be the Griefers, the ones that work for the queen—the one behind all this. The higher someone's role is, the more powerful their chess piece," said Junior.

"And I have a name for these people," Silvis said. "I call them Wild Cards."

"Interesting name. I like it," Ghost complimented him.

"We need to catch these pawns—wild cards," Silvis said.

"And how are we supposed to do that?" Elly asked.

"Junior." Silvis stared into Junior's brown eyes. "House. Elevator."
Junior looked confused, and then he nodded and a grin spread across his face wider. Everyone else looked confused, but Silvis and Junior ignored them.

"We'll be right back!" said Junior.

•

Twenty minutes later they were in Junior's house. "How'd you open it?" Junior asked Silvis, staring at the wall with the elevator.

"I just bumped into it. Honest!"

"Hmm."

"What did you see down there?" Junior asked.

"Nothing, really. Weird stuff. I saw a painting or something. Couldn't make out what it was." Silvis must've been talking too casually because Junior raised an eyebrow for a split second. Silvis wasn't a good liar because there was nobody to lie to all these years that he was alone. He didn't want Junior to feel bad or think that he looked through his stuff.

Junior was about to place his hand on a certain part of the wall when he froze. "Wait, what's that?" Junior pointed to a little dent right where he was going to put his hand.

"I think that's where I hit my head," Silvis said.

"Wow. You hit your head in the exact place where the hidden button is," said Junior. He placed his hand on the spot with the dent, and it was like magic. The wall shifted to one side and turned into an elevator. They both stepped inside. "That's lucky."

Ding! The elevator doors slid open. The room was beautiful and mysterious, like he had seen before.

Junior walked to a corner and Silvis followed. He picked up a weird camera that looked like a sensor.

"What's that?" Silvis asked.

"It's a thermal heat sensor. It can sense heat. See, look." Junior pointed the sensor at his body. "See how my body looks orange and red? That means my body temperature is hot. If something is orange and red, that means it's warm or hot. We can use this to track down pawns—wild cards."

"Smart idea," Silvis replied.

"Oh, and look here. There's a magnifying glass, invisible ink and a quill, a camera for evidence, a printer for even more evidence, a flashlight, a ski mask, a black morph suit, a confetti blast—"

Silvis grabbed Junior's arm. "Wait, what the heck is a confetti blaster?"

Junior glared at Silvis's hand on his arm until Silvis dropped it. Then Junior met Silvis's eyes. "A blaster that shoots confetti," he said flatly, as if everyone should know this information.

"Oh," said Silvis.

"Anyways, there's a pocketknife, taser, brush, and a rope. You think that'll be enough?"

"More than enough."

Silvis walked over to the elevator, but Junior stopped. He picked up a picture of a young boy.

"Who's that?" Silvis said, interrupting Junior's thoughts.

Junior jumped up and shoved the painting behind his back.

"Oh, sorry, I—" said Silvis.

"No, it's fine," Junior said. "It's Bear when he was ten."

"Oh."

"We should get going," Junior added.

Silvis didn't say a word but nodded his head and then stepped into the elevator. Junior stepped in, too, carrying a bag full of the supplies.

•

Twenty minutes later, Junior dumped all the supplies down in front of the others at Newberry Park.

"Where the heck did you get all this stuff?" Elly asked in amazement.

Ghost lifted an eyebrow as if he were kind of impressed.

Elly turned to Silvis. "And what's with that elevator talk?"

"It's our secret," Junior replied.

A large gust of wind smacked all their faces, and someone sneezed loudly. Everyone turned to see a figure running away.

"What the—where in the—hey, get back here!" Junior yelled. He threw a camera at Silvis, which Silvis quickly put around his neck. Silvis grabbed an airsoft pistol from his pocket and ran after the figure.

Behind him, Silvis heard Elly say, "You carry that with you everywhere?"

He chuckled for a moment and kept running. Junior was not far behind Silvis, holding a rope, a magnifying glass, and a flashlight, even though it was afternoon. The figure, who was dressed in black from head to toe and looked around Silvis's age, ran into an alleyway that was next to the park and a busy road.

The alleyway was very dark and spooky. All of a sudden, it felt like it was midnight. The figure seemed to have disappeared.

"Shh," Junior said. There was an abandoned warehouse, a spooky apartment building which had stairs to the roof, and an old, abandoned antique shop. As Silvis and Junior scanned the area, a flowerpot fell from the apartment building and nearly hit them. The flowerpot hit the ground and shattered into pieces.

They craned their heads above them and saw the figure at one of the highest apartment rooms. They could see him more clearly now: He was wearing a black morph suit and he had a mini camera attached to his head. He immediately started running up flights of stairs, and Silvis and Junior ran after him. They were faster than him, but he still got to the roof before them. He began running to the end of the building. There was a building a few feet away from the apartment and, to Silvis, it seemed like he was going to jump onto it. The figure glanced back for a few seconds, right as he was reaching the end of the building.

Then he hit his knee on a brick wall. "OW!" he screamed, and he held his knee in pain. He hopped on one foot, and Silvis and Junior caught up to him.

But he slipped off the edge of the building, holding onto a brick that was sticking out. He started losing grip and he yelled, "Help me!"

Junior quickly threw the rope down to the kid in the morph suit and he grabbed hold of it. Silvis and Junior pulled the rope up until the kid was back on the roof. The kid sat up, but before he could make a move, Junior pinned him to the ground, put the rope around him, and tied him to a pole. The kid struggled but couldn't get out.

"Why are you here? Who sent you? What do you want?" Junior asked.

"Why should I tell you?" the kid muttered.

Silvis pulled out his airsoft pistol from behind his back and aimed it at the kid. "Tell us or else ..."

"Okay, okay. I'm one of the pawns, as you call them. The Master sent me as a spy. But you'll never catch the Master, even if you catch all the pawns."

"Silvis, take a picture of him for evidence."

Silvis quickly grabbed the camera and snapped a picture of the kid. "Ha! We'll get 'em all in no time!" he said, jumping into the air with glee.

"That's right," Junior added and continued to question. "Now tell me—"

CLANG!

"What is that? Looks like some alien device ..." said Junior.

On the ground next to them was an odd, green camouflage cylinder made of a metal-like material with an oversized trigger on top of it. Suddenly, Junior realized what it was. "Wait a minute, that's a—"

BOOM!

It was too late. Smoke filled the air and covered everything in Silvis and Junior's sight. They coughed and coughed. There was too much smoke for them to see, and they were inhaling too much of it to try to escape. Thirty miserable seconds later, the smoke faded away and Silvis and Junior coughed hard, thankful to be inhaling air again.

The pawn was gone, the ropes cut open. Silvis stared at the ropes in disbelief.

"At least we got a picture," said Junior, trying to sound as optimistic as possible.

"I'm just thankful to be alive," said Silvis.

Junior and Silvis walked back to the park with the supplies.

"So?" said Ghost impatiently.

"Well, er—" Silvis didn't know what to say. He knew they would all be extremely disappointed.

"Lemme guess ..." Ghost said. "You lost him?"

"It's more complicated than that. If I told you the truth, you guys would think we're crazy."

"C'mon ..." pleaded Willow. "Just tell us. I promise I'll believe you."

"Okay," Silvis agreed. "We chased the guy down on top of an apartment building and then he was about to fall off, but Junior saved him with his rope. Honestly, I wish we hadn't saved him. Then we tied him up. I was able to get a picture ... then all of a sudden, *poof!* A smoke grenade appears, and next thing I know, Junior and I are coughing and begging for air! And the guy escaped! His ropes were cut free and he was nowhere in sight. In all the chaos, after the smoke cleared, we forgot to check the surroundings. Also, we got a few answers from that guy. He says he's a spy and a pawn. He called the wild card leading them all the Master."

"I've seen many odd things, but a smoke bomb! We're just kids! The person who threw that must be a kid too!" said Willow.

"Yeah, well, it's the truth," said Silvis.

Everyone believed Junior and Silvis except for Ghost, who was suspicious about the smoke bomb.

Silvis was tired. He was tired of all the trouble and complications in the case, but he knew that he couldn't quit, not this far into it. Just the feeling of not solving the case and letting the wild cards roam free and causing more havoc sent chills down Silvis's spine. *You can do this, Silvis,* he thought to himself.

•

Thirty minutes later, Silvis arrived at his house. Polo had made a mess again, but it was worth it. He couldn't have afforded Polo bothering him in the meeting and slowing him down on the bike rides. Once again, Silvis was exhausted. All the stress of losing the spy surged through his mind, like a stampede of buffaloes rampaging through his head. Thoughts about the case just wouldn't leave his mind. He knew sleeping was the best option.

Ignoring Polo and the mess in the house, Silvis rushed up to his room and slammed the door shut. He fell asleep immediately.

•

Beep! Beep!

"Shut up ..." said Silvis gloomily.

Beep! Beep!

"Shut it!"

Beep! Beep!

Silvis sprang up from his bed. It was the alarm clock. Why was it waking him up so early? Silvis turned off the annoying clock. It was 7:20 A.M. and...

"Monday!" he shouted. He had to go to school. He wanted to dig his body into the bedsheets and sleep forever, but he knew he couldn't. With a sigh, he got up.

Silvis packed a penne pasta that Polo made into his backpack. It reminded him of the delicious food his mom used to cook. Thinking of his mom made him shiver. Trying to forget, he walked out the door with his bike.

While biking, he remembered his dream. Something was being burnt. It was an instrument... a violin or guitar, probably. Flames circled the instrument, and then the memory ended. It felt awfully realistic.

Silvis loved violins. His mother taught him how to play, and her lessons were much better than the music class he attended. They used to have a whole collection in their house, but the violins disappeared when his parents disappeared.

Maybe what he saw in the dream was real. Maybe it was a memory. Silvis always wanted a violin, but he didn't have too much money and he wasn't going to blow a whole bunch of it on a violin.

He finally made it to school and locked his bike. Then he walked toward the front gate.

"Name?" asked Mr. Herman, standing straight and tall at the gate. He peered down at Silvis while scratching something on his clipboard.

"Silvis Wren," Silvis replied.

Mr. Herman scanned his long list of names, then said, "You can go." Silvis scanned his card and walked through the gates. Junior and Ghost were waiting.

"Silvis," said Ghost.

"Yeah?" Silvis answered.

"We've found something."

"What is it?"

"It's about the kids who were drugged, remember? They haven't said a word to anyone, and no one knows what's going on. The hospital and government said I can visit and talk to the kids. The invitation said I can bring anyone who's working with me, so you guys can come," said Junior.

"Oh," said Silvis, who was losing interest in the case after yesterday. He hadn't stopped scolding himself for losing the spy.

"Meet me at the swings after school," said Junior as he walked off to get to class.

Silvis sighed. This case was too much. He had already gotten himself too deep into it, and he couldn't quit. He still had no idea where Zak was, the Griefgins made him shiver, and there were Wild Cards out on the loose. Silvis slipped on his backpack, which he had set down while listening to Junior and Ghost, and walked to his classroom.

School was pretty normal—easy because it was the beginning of the year. During social studies, Junior, whose desk was on the far right of the classroom, got up to sharpen his pencil. When he crossed Silvis's desk, which was in the center of the classroom, he dropped a note. Silvis heard Junior sharpen his pencil for a couple seconds and walk back to his desk.

Silvis snuck a peek at the note:

There's a Wild Card somewhere; I've found something!

Why didn't he write what the clue was? Silvis thought.

Mrs. Coral's voice broke the silence, "Silvis, is that a note I see?"

"Wha—er—oh—" said Silvis, startled and embarrassed.

Before Silvis could give a full answer, Mrs. Coral said, "Please give me that note. Passing notes is not allowed. This is just a warning for you, but if anyone is passing notes again, then there will be consequences."

Mrs. Coral suddenly seemed very strict, even though she had only given him a warning. Embarrassed, Silvis walked up to Mrs. Coral, who was next to the white board. Silvis gave the note to Mrs. Coral and walked back to his desk, trying not to see all the kids staring at him and whispering.

To Silvis's horror, Mrs. Coral began to read the note out loud. "'There's a Wild Card somewhere'... Wild Card?" Mrs. Coral continued reading, "'I've found something.' Very odd," she muttered as she threw the note in the trash bin.

Silvis heard snickering and whispering all around him.

"Quiet down, class!" said Mrs. Coral, and they all got back to work.

At recess, Silvis grabbed his homemade cookie and began walking to the benches. After ten minutes of enjoying his pasta all alone, Junior ran up to him.

"Silvis, I'm sorry for giving you the note," said Junior. "I didn't mean for you to get in trouble."

"It's alright," Silvis replied.

"Okay, this is important."

"What is it?"

"Have you seen the poster?"

"What poster?"

Junior pointed to a wall.

Behind Junior's detective stand was a wall, large and visible to everyone, with a poster stuck to it. The poster was huge, and when Silvis read it, his jaws dropped open.

The New Detective is Here!

An exclusive kid detective for Hillstretch Elementary has been hired to replace the last detective. Detective Charlie is here to solve the case of the Griefings!

A rush of panic, confusion, and anger rushed through Silvis. Tons of questions went through his mind, but the only thing that came out of his mouth was, "Why?"

"I know," said Junior.

Silvis felt like screaming a bunch of horrible words at the new detective, but he resisted the feeling. "Why would Mr. Williams replace you with this fool?!" Silvis yelled, making the crowd of kids next to the poster stare at him in awkward silence.

The poster had a picture of the new detective, Charlie, on it. He had straight combed hair and he was extremely short. He wore a detective hat that was way too big for him and overalls on top of a striped black shirt.

After a moment, the kids' attention went away from him and back to discussing the situation. But all at once, they stopped speaking and looked at something behind them.

A high-pitched childish voice said, "Did someone just call me a fool?"

Silvis and Junior looked back to see the new detective, Charlie, staring at them. Beside him were two tall and buff kids wearing black tank tops with skulls on them and black shorts. Everyone knew these two boys known as the Terror Twins. They were the biggest bullies in the school, and everyone feared them.

Fear seized Silvis. Everyone said that those who the Terror Twins didn't like would always have an imprint from them. But Silvis shifted from frightened to curious. Why would the biggest bullies in the school be with Charlie, who was the type of person they would beat up and embarrass at first sight?

The Terror Twins were staring menacingly at Silvis and Junior when all of sudden Charlie said, "Ah, it's the old detective... You're pretty horrible at solving cases. That's why Mr. Williams fired you!" he said, trying to sound fierce but still having his same childish voice. Then he burst into laughter.

"We're gonna get you!" said one of the Terror Twins.

Junior and Silvis walked away discouraged and hopeless, again.

CHAPTER 6

HOSPITAL

All day, Silvis and Junior had feared that the Terror Twins would attack them. But Junior had arranged some clear tape in between two trees, and the twins had run straight into it. They hit their heads so hard that they had to go to the nurse's office for the rest of the school day.

Silvis and Junior walked out of the Hillstretch Elementary gates, relieved that they had escaped the Terror Twins. "They may have muscles, but they don't have brains," Junior said. Silvis burst into laughter.

Junior's meeting with the drugged kids was in an hour and a half. The Hillstretch Hospital was in the city, which Silvis rarely went to. Ghost had his motorcycle, so he had said that he'd meet them in their chosen meeting spot, outside the city's most popular hotel. Elly had texted Junior on his computer that she'd made an excuse and told her mom she was going shopping in the city, so her mom would drop her off at the meeting spot. Silvis was going to bike, Junior would ride his Segway, and Willow was going to walk.

"Alright, we should get going," said Junior.

Silvis biked back to his house, where Polo, who had made a mess yet again, was waiting. "Darn it!" muttered Silvis.

Polo was digging through a pile of clothes that just come out of the laundry and he stopped when he heard Silvis walk in. "Silvis," Polo said, staring at him with a face full of guilt.

Silvis didn't have time to deal with Polo. He simply scowled at him and walked up the stairs. He ate some toast that he maybe toasted a little too much, then stuffed an airsoft pistol in his pocket. But then he realized that an airsoft gun probably wouldn't be allowed in a hospital, so he put it back. Silvis brought an apple with him in case he got hungry and put Polo in his cradle in hopes that he would fall asleep (although it was doubtful).

Silvis walked out of his house and began biking to the hospital. It was a long way, about an hour, but he didn't mind. He figured Junior would probably bring a camera and any other detective tools he needed, so Silvis didn't need to worry about supplies.

On his way to the city, Silvis saw many kids walking home from school. He was surprised he didn't see Willow on the way, but he figured she probably started walking immediately after school ended. Some people pointed, whispered, and stared when he passed by. Everyone probably knew what had happened at recess by now, but Silvis didn't care about what others thought of him. *We'll see who's laughing when we solve this case,* he thought, though deep down, he wasn't sure they ever would. *At least we're putting effort into it.*

Silvis finally arrived outside of the hotel an hour later, where Junior, Ghost, and Willow were waiting.

"Hey, Silvis," Ghost said.

"Hi, guys," Silvis said, putting his bike in a bike rack. "So, how come Elly isn't here yet? Wasn't her mom supposed to be driving her here?"

"I don't know why she's not here yet, but she better be here soon, or we'll be late for the meeting," said Willow. "Also, we heard what happened at recess."

Silvis nodded. He didn't want to talk about it because it was quite embarrassing, but these were his friends. "I still don't understand why the Terror Twins are helping Charlie."

"Well, it's quite simple," said Junior.

"What do you mean?" said Silvis.

"Well, the Terror Twins have to be Wild Cards. They were after us all day at school."

"What's that got to do with them helping Charlie?"

"Charlie is an idiot. He's a horrible detective, I know it for sure. The Terror

Twins know he's an idiot and they're helping him because he's a bad detective. They're Wild Cards, and they want a bad detective so the case doesn't get solved. Simple as that," Junior explained with a grin.

The conclusion was so simple for Junior, but Silvis would've never thought of it. Everyone was silent for a moment, shocked by how (and when) Junior had thought of all this.

"We're gonna be late; Elly better show up soon," said Ghost, looking at his watch.

Sure enough, a moment later, there was a screech of tires and Elly's car rolled up. "Bye, honey!" her mom called. Willow snickered. Elly slammed the door shut and walked towards them.

"What took you so long?" Ghost asked.

Elly rolled her eyes and put her hands on her hips. "My mom wanted me to go to her friend's houseto meet his son, who is a nasty little fool. He's, like, five or something, and he all he wanted to do was play with his toy trucks. And then he tried trippping me. And then he started crying when I didn't do what he wanted. A real brat."

"Well, let's get going now!" Ghost said.

Silvis, Junior, Ghost, Elly, and Willow began walking to the hospital. Elly wanted to look in some stores on the way, which delayed them quite a bit. Finally, after about ten minutes, they arrived at the Hillstretch Hospital. When they entered the hospital, Junior was immediately recognized by a lady who was at the registration desk.

"Oh, hello!" the lady called. "You must be the detective coming here for the meeting!"

"Yep," Junior replied. "And these are my friends who have come with me. They're helping me investigate." He had his pipe in his mouth, blowing out bubbles. Everyone around the room stared at the five them.

"Right, well, come on, I'll take you there," the lady said.

They followed the lady to an elevator and walked in. The lady pressed the sixth floor button, and the elevator began to go up.

Ding! The elevator doors swung open. In front of them was a sitting room with many parents and children waiting. There was a registration area, too.

The lady led them down a hall with pictures of the staff members on the walls and some rooms. The lady opened a door and went into an area with many hospital rooms. They walked up to a doctor, who was talking to a nurse. The nurse finished saying something and walked away.

"Hi, Derik, this is the detective and his friends who are helping him," the lady said.

Derik was a tall man with a brown beard and messy hair. "Hello, there! I'm Doctor Derik!" He shook Junior's hand with a very strong grip. "Come on, I'll show you the patients," he said, and he began walking to a hospital room. He knocked on the door twice and then opened it. Inside were two nurses talking to each other and two boys lying on their hospital beds with IV bags poked into their arms.

"Boys: this is the detective and his friends!" Derik said.

The two nurses stopped talking and looked at the five kids. One of the nurses said, "Here are the boys, they're quite healthy now but still affected by the sleeping gas. We don't want to send them home until they start speaking."

The nurses stepped aside, and Junior, Silvis, Willow, Elly, and Ghost walked closer to the injured boys. They were clearly awake; their eyes were wide open and they were staring at Junior, who was in the front of the group. Their gaze shifted over to the rest of the kids and then back to Junior when he cleared his throat.

"Hello," Junior said. He waited a moment, and when they didn't reply, he continued, "My name is Junior, and I'm a kid detective. I'm here to talk to you and ask you a few questions."

The two boys simply stared at Junior with an expression of curiosity. It seemed like they wanted to reply but they just couldn't.

The five kids waited in silence for a few more seconds. Ghost blurted, "Well, it doesn't seem like this is working."

The boys shot Ghost a hard glance. Ghost sighed and turned for the door. For some odd reason, Silvis had never thought that the boys wouldn't respond and that their plan wouldn't work.

Silvis lost all his hope and he was ready to leave. Suddenly, the unmistakable voice of Junior said, "Wait!"

Everyone, who was now at the door, stopped and locked their eyes on Junior. Even the boys stared at him.

"Um," Junior began, "Maybe they'll talk if you guys leave the room?" His eyes were on the doctor and nurses.

Doctor Derik and the nurses exchanged looks and then Derik said, "For the boys' safety, we normally wouldn't leave them alone with others they don't know, but I trust you guys to stay."

Silvis hadn't thought of talking to them alone, but it seemed like a good idea.

"We'll be outside or in the hallway if you need anything," said the doctor.

Junior nodded. Derik and the nurses left the room, the door swinging closed. Silvis was sure this wasn't going to work, but it was worth a try. The boy's eyes were once again looking at the kids with that same look, as if they wanted to say something.

"Hello," Junior began. "As I said, I'm a kid detective and I'm—"

"Yeah, we know," one of the boys said before Junior could finish.

Silvis gasped and jumped back in surprise. Elly nearly screamed, but Ghost clamped his hand over her mouth and jumped backwards, almost tripping on the IV. Willow jumped back and also almost tripped. Junior's eyes widened, but he didn't have a crazy reaction.

"Wow," Junior muttered. "Never expected that to work."

"Hi," the other boy said. "I'm Verse and this is my best friend, Grady."

"Nice to meet you," Junior replied. "So, it seems that you're talking, huh."

"Yes," Grady said.

"Why is that?"

"Because you're a detective. We trust you, and hopefully, your friends are trustworthy, too." He eyed them suspiciously and then shifted his gaze back to Junior.

"As I said, I have a few questions," said Junior. "Firstly, why are you not speaking to anyone except us? You don't even speak to your family or the doctors and nurses, who can help you a lot. Did the sleeping gas have some effect that made you not be able to talk? Did Ghast force you not to say anything?"

"Ghast?" echoed Elly, with a very suspicious look. "Who's that?"

"Oh, nobody. Sorry."

Elly didn't say anything more, but she still seemed suspicious about it.

"Wait," said Grady. "What do you mean by sleeping gas? That big scary guy with the creepy mask attacked us and broke our arms."

"Broke your arms? Oh, no, nothing happened to your arms. You were given sleeping gas or sleeping pills."

"No!" Verse shouted. "No! No! I know that our arms are broken! I can't feel it, but I just know it! They're broken, they're broken!" Grady shouted.

"That's weird," Junior whispered loudly. "The sleeping gas or pills they were given made them think their arms were broken. Well, the effects should wear off soon, but that's weird. Why would—I mean, yeah, why would the creepy guy want them to think he broke their arms? Anyways, can one of you tell me what happened when you were drugged—I mean, attacked?"

"We were out on a walk to the park, but then I saw a tie on the ground under some trees. No one was around, and I wanted to see what it was doing there, so I walked up to it. And suddenly, I saw some big tall guy wearing a mask with two X's on it running towards me. He was holding something big and metal. I screamed, and Verse came running to me and he saw the guy. Before we could run, the guy hit our arms hard with the metal thing and everything went dark. The last thing I saw was Verse's eyes closing."

Junior stood there for a moment and then muttered, "A trap."

"What?" Silvis said. *What is Junior talking about?*

"That was no coincidence," Junior said. "It was a setup. The guy was waiting for them, he knew they were coming."

"Does that mean he was watching us?" Verse asked.

"Yes. He was spying on you guys. For how long I don't know, but I have no idea why he cared about you guys," said Junior.

It seemed like everyone was thinking for a moment. Silvis couldn't come up with anything, though. Then Junior said, "Hold on!"

"What?" Ghost asked.

"Grady, Verse, did you see anything weird in the few weeks before you were attacked?" Junior questioned.

"Well, Verse got a letter," Grady told them.

"What kind of letter? What did it say?" Silvis asked.

"It was very weird. It said it was from 'your local crime organization.' It was inviting Verse to help them with a big event where they were gonna cause havoc," said Grady.

"They said I would probably accept, and if I did, I should meet them at midnight in Newberry Park," Verse explained.

Silvis felt chills going down his spine. *A crime group inviting third-graders to help them? Could it possibly be the Wild Cards?*

Silvis's thoughts were interrupted by Junior asking, "And what did you do?"

"I love being mischievous, but the crime part scared me. I didn't want to do any crime or help criminals. Also, going to meet people who I don't even know at midnight sounds creepy. I showed it to Grady, and he told me not to go, so I ended up not going."

"Aha!" cheered Junior triumphantly.

"What?" Willow asked. "Am I the only one who never understands Junior?"

They all chuckled for a moment but then Junior interrupted them by saying, "It all makes sense."

They stared at Junior, expecting a long and great explanation. "The group which invited Verse, 'your local criminal organization,' as it's called, are the Wild Cards. They invited Verse, knowing that he loved mischief and havoc. The so-called 'event' was the Griefings, and they wanted him to be part of it. They expected that Verse would accept the invitation and become a wild card, but to their surprise, it actually freaked him out. You made the right decision, Verse. The people who invited you were the ones behind the Griefings." He smiled broadly at Verse and then continued, "They knew Verse knew too much, and so they sent Gha—I mean, the creepy guy—to spy on them. But the Wild Cards found out that Grady knew about the invitation too, and so they told the creepy guy to attack him, too. I believe he gave you a drug so you would forget about the invitation but weirdly, instead, it made you guys think your arms broke."

This was a lot to process. Silvis still understood what Junior was trying to say, though.

"So," Junior continued. "Where was this letter sent and what was it sent in?"

"It was in a plain white envelope with my name on it and the word 'mischief' but nothing else. I found it in my backpack. I have no idea how it got there," Verse said.

"Very interesting," Junior muttered to himself. "A plain white envelope with the words 'mischief.' The envelope was put in his backpack by a wild card at the school. Not a surprise, considering that most Wild Cards are probably kids at the school. Be on the lookout for these envelopes, or any clues about them. The Wild Cards may have hints to what they're planning nex—"

"What are the Wild Cards?" Grady blurted. It seemed like he didn't want to interrupt Junior's explanations, but the words just slipped out of his mouth.

"Oh," Junior said, hesitating for a moment. "They're the people who caused the Griefings."

Elly cleared her throat, slipping her phone into her pocket. She had said nothing up to now. "So, was any of that important?"

Everyone stared at her for a second, and then Willow hissed, "Well, duh! Didn't you hear what the boys said and Junior's long explanations?"

"Umm," Elly replied, embarrassed.

"I—you—" Willow gasped. "THOSE KIDS WERE SAYING IMPORTANT, CRITICAL INFORMATION AND JUNIOR DID HIS LONG EXPLANATION ABOUT WHY THEY WERE ATTACKED AND YOU WERE ON YOUR PHONE THE WHOLE TIME!"

"Er—" Elly began.

"Save it!" Willow yelled.

The boys laughed. Elly glared at them for a moment and then looked away. "So, uh, what exactly happened?" Elly asked, her voice dripping with guilt.

It felt like an eternity later when Junior finally finished explaining what had happened—again. She tried acting surprised and curious about many things that Junior said, but it was quite clear to them all that she didn't find any of it amusing and she would've much rather been on her phone. At least she had listened (or appeared to listen).

They got ready to leave. Then Junior blurted, "I'm sorry, but I don't want to keep anything from you guys. This was all recorded on the security cameras."

Verse and Grady replied at the same time, "Actually, it's not."

"What do you mean?"

"Whenever visitors come in and visit us, the cameras get disabled. I think whoever is doing that thinks I might talk, and they don't want me to tell anyone what happened," said Verse.

"That doesn't make any sense," said Ghost.

"Wait, does that mean—" Silvis started.

Junior finished for him. "Yep, it's the Wild Cards. They hacked the security cameras just in case the boys told anyone anything, so there's no evidence." His voice was full of disappointment.

"What's so bad about that?" Silvis asked.

"We don't have evidence. Without evidence, we could tell authorities all about what we were told, but they couldn't know that what we said was true. The cameras had all the evidence, all of our proof. But now there's no proof," he said dimly.

Things were looking bad for the young detectives.

CHAPTER 7

DETECTIVE CHALLENGE

The rest of the week was terrible for Silvis and Junior. It wasn't just the pressure of upcoming tests (which were easy for Junior but hard for Silvis)—it was primarily concerning the new detective, Charlie.

Charlie had been wriggling his way out of all the questions about the case he was being asked. It was obvious to Junior that he wasn't conducting any investigating, and if he was, he wasn't finding any clues. Junior, on the other hand, was being made fun of because everyone thought that he had been kicked out of the detective role for the school.

Everyone thinks Junior is worse than Charlie, Silvis thought. *But how can he be worse than Charlie when there is nothing worse than Charlie?*

Charlie kept sending the Terror Twins to taunt, bother, and annoy Silvis and Junior (mostly Junior), as well as spread rumors, like, "Junior wasn't solving the case," "He's not even a real detective! He's a fraud! He's a fraud!" and "He was actually part of the Griefings, he's a criminal!" People believed them enough to think that Junior was some sort of crazy kid. (At one point, Elly asked if one of the rumors were true and Willow glared at her).

Ever since the argument at the hospital, Willow was hardly talking to Elly and trying to avoid any conversations with her. Willow's foul behavior seemed to convince people at school, who seemed to believe the rumors. As much as she tried to convince people they were fake and that Charlie was a horrible detective, no one seemed to listen.

It was a terrible week, and pretty soon, people were finding out who Junior's friends were and staying away from them. People had already thought of Silvis as weird—ever since the first day of school—but now everyone shot him dirty looks.

Silvis was used to used to this type of behavior, but he didn't like it. Since nobody saw him with parents or a family, people made fun of him being an orphan or a street kid.

But going back to school had changed everything. Made him feel hope again. He finally had friends and felt like kids his own age.

Not anymore. This was worse than before, and now he just felt like the same old orphan that no one wanted to go near.

"Hey, guys, how's the case coming along?" Charlie's sinister voice said at recess one day. "Oh, wait. You're just an orphan without a brain and you're a fake detective. Two failures. Yeah, foster kid, I'm going to tell everyone who you really are," he said with a chuckle of delight.

That can't be, Silvis thought. *How does Charlie know? I'd be doomed if everyone knew who I really was.*

"No!" Silvis yelled. With no signs of guilt or a hint of any kind of sympathy, Charlie just sat there and smiled evilly. *Charlie is probably the most evil kid on the planet,* Silvis thought. *Is he the Master of the Wild Cards? The one behind it all? But he can't be! He's so dumb and stupid. The only thing he does know is how to annoy someone to death.*

"So, Silvis, your time of existence in this school has come to an end." He picked his nose foolishly.

Charlie was right. Silvis was doomed, and there was nothing he could do. Charlie spared them an hour before he would tell the whole school. Silvis was sure there was no way to outsmart Charlie. Junior spent every moment he had brainstorming, but even he couldn't think of anything.

It felt like an eternity before the hour finally passed by, giving Silvis every moment to worry about what would happen next. At least he doesn't know where you live, he told himself, trying to have some positivity.

He would be kicked out of school and sent away to some orphanage, which seemed like the worst possible thing. He liked school, he liked where he lived. Most people thought his house was abandoned, and since Silvis always had his curtains up, people couldn't see the lights or anyone in the house. (But some people had seen the lights before and thought the house was haunted with a ghost living in it. Silvis always chuckled when he thought about it.)

He heard lots of kids running. Charlie was standing on top of a desk in the middle of the blacktop. Charlie did these types of things all the time, and the staff and teachers never seemed to care or say anything at all.

But now was Silvis's time of doom, and Junior was nowhere to be seen. *Maybe he doesn't want to be around me now that I'm about to be exposed.* He felt like crying, but he held back the tears. Instead, he let all his horrible thoughts and sadness wash through his mind. His heart thumped faster and faster, singing its own sad tune. Silvis took a deep breath. Maybe he didn't need to live this kind of life... Maybe he could ditch school and run away, to somewhere else, where he could have a fresh start.

He was seriously considering it until Junior and Willow and his other friends came into his mind. He imagined them wondering where he went (though he wasn't sure if Elly would care). Snap out of it, he scolded himself. *They're your only friends and possibly the only friends you'll ever have.* He was ready to face his doom.

"So," Charlie sneered, "it has come to my attention that someone here has been lying to us about something. Someone who has been acting like they're normal when they really aren't." His smile shifted over to Silvis, whose face flushed red.

The crowd burst into conversation, and it was clear that they all thought Charlie had figured out something about the Griefings. *How could they ever think that lump of idiocy could come up with anything?*

Charlie cleared his throat, and everyone stopped talking, waiting to hear the information. He opened his mouth, but Junior's confident voice yelled above the crowd, "Wait!"

Bewildered, everyone suddenly locked their eyes on Junior.

"What do you want, filthy fraud?!" Charlie hissed.

Junior stared at him with confidence. "I am no fraud. And what he's talking about has nothing to do with the case. Just more unfounded rumors and lies he's made up."

Charlie's eyes widened.

What is Junior doing? Why would he be standing up to Charlie? Now, he's embarrassed himself, and we'll both be even bigger idiots. Silvis felt the urge to shout at Junior, but he didn't dare to say anything. If Charlie's attention returned to Silvis, it might reveal his secret.

"What are you trying to say?" Charlie asked. "Is this a trick? An ambush? Are you stalling me or distracting me?"

"Actually," Junior said triumphantly. "I'm here to challenge you."

"What challenge?" said Charlie with a hint of fear in his voice.

"I challenge you to a *detective* challenge. The rules are simple. We have a whole week to find a clue, or as many clues as we can, about the Griefings. Whoever finds the most clues wins. We shall discuss which clues we found and who did better on Friday, and to make it fair, the audience can decide the winner. But if I win, then you shall no longer make up any more lies and rumors, including the one you're about to say, or boast about you being a better detective. It'll be quite clear who's the better detective." Junior grinned, saying each word with delight.

At first, Silvis was shocked. How could Junior come up with something that genius? They were sure to win because Charlie was not a good detective. But then it struck him: *What if the Wild Cards told Charlie some clues? He would surely win, wouldn't he?*

Charlie tried to hide how worried he was, but the fear was all over him. He was shivering and his mouth dropped open. His eyes looked like tears would spill out at any moment.

"So, Charlie, do you accept my challenge? I mean, you are a much better detective than me according to your wonderful self, right? Surely, you could easily beat me, right?"

The crowd let out their bursts of laughter and Charlie looked away from them nervously. They stopped laughing after the Terror Twins gave them all menacing glares. Still shivering, Charlie managed to say, "Er, I—well—um—"

"Charlie? You aren't scared, are you? You aren't worried I might beat you?"

"Um—er, n-no, of c-course not ..."

"Oh, so if you're not scared, then do you accept the challenge?"

"Um—y-y-yeah, I-I accept," he managed to say before pretending to sneeze. "Yeah, I'll s-see you guys l-later." And then he ran off.

"Junior!" Silvis cried. "Thank you so much! That was genius!"

Junior grinned broadly. "No problem."

"But there is one problem."

"What?"

"Well, wouldn't the Wild Cards tell Charlie a few clues to make sure he wins?" Silvis said desperately.

Junior kept smiling. "No, silly. There are many flaws to what you just said. First of all, the Wild Cards wouldn't reveal anything that would help detectives. Secondly, Charlie isn't a Wild Card, and he doesn't even know that the Terror Twins are Wild Cards either. He just thinks that everyone likes him. And also, the Wild Cards have no reason to help Charlie at all. Why would they care about some contest that's working against them and doesn't affect them?"

At first it was confusing, but then it all clicked in Silvis's mind. How did he not realize that? Silvis grinned back at Junior. "Didn't think of that."

The day had gone from absolutely miserable to surprisingly great. Silvis couldn't help himself from imagining the look on Charlie's face on Friday.

•

When school was over, Silvis went home and dealt with Polo, who, after some time, snuck away somewhere. Silvis spent half an hour finishing up his homework and then watched some TV. Everything felt perfectly normal until he heard a creak from upstairs. *Ugh. What's my crazy monkey up to, now?*

"Polo!" he screeched. He heard someone running, but it wasn't an ape.

It was definitely a human. Silvis was filled with fear, but he knew what must be done. He bolted up the stairs and saw the door to his room was open. He braced himself, ready for a fight. Without a moment more of hesitation, he ran into the room, ready to charge into whoever was in his house.

But no one was there. Silvis's window was open. He had stuck his head out a few hours earlier to feel the breeze and breathe some fresh air, but he must've forgotten to lock it. *Whoever broke in left behind no trace except the window being open.* But then Silvis turned around and saw his computer. It was open, and he had not left it open. His computer contained all his messages with Junior.

Whoever broke in was looking at my messages with Junior. Why would they want to see my messages? Why would they break in just to see the messages? Or were they doing something else?

He was glad the messages didn't say much about the case. But then Silvis looked at the messages and saw that Junior had sent him two new ones. The first read: "Hey Silvis, I'm planning on starting to investigate and it would be great if you came along." The second one said: "When can you meet me? Tell me that first, then I'll tell you where to meet."

Silvis forgot about the break-in for a moment and started thinking about the case but then soon realized what he really needed.

"Junior!" he said. Junior was the key! Silvis texted Junior what had happened. Within seconds, Junior replied that he'd be at Silvis's house in a moment. Silvis double-checked and locked every door, window, or possible entrance to the house, then waited, worried that something else could happen.

Junior rang the doorbell twenty minutes later. When Silvis opened the door, he was bombarded with questions.

"Are you alright? Are you hurt? Did you see who broke in?"

"Junior!" Silvis said impatiently.

"What?"

"I'm fine."

"I have come to a conclusion."

"Really? That fast?"

"Yes."

"What is it?"

"Your house was broken into by Wild Cards. No one else would have any interest in breaking into your house just to check your messages. So, you obviously remember what happened at the hospital, right? Well, the security cameras were hacked by Wild Cards, who disabled them to get rid of evidence. They know we heard a lot; they just don't know what. That's exactly why they came. It may seem like they broke in to attack you or get answers from you, but they were smart and careful. They know we know too much, but they wanted to see just how much we know. They're being careful not to be caught, so they checked our messages for if we'd said anything about the clues we've found. Luckily, there was nothing important in the messages."

"That makes a lot of sense. It still freaks me out that someone was in my house. And it's frustrating that the Wild Cards are onto us! It's like they're one step ahead," said Silvis.

"They are, but not for long. We're getting closer to cracking the case every day."

After having a snack, Junior and Silvis headed upstairs to look for any remaining clues from the break-in. "Alright, let's see..." Junior said, pulling out his magnifying glass. He studied all the halls, just in case, for what felt like ages.

Suddenly, he said, "Aha!"

Silvis jumped up in surprise. Both of them were so focused that they hadn't spoken since they started looking. Silvis hadn't expected to find anything, either.

"What!" Silvis said desperately.

"I found it. Footprints."

Silvis ran over to Junior and saw it: right in front of his desk were four large footprints.

"These are their footprints from when they were looking at the messages!" Silvis gasped.

"Yes," Junior agreed. "There were two people. As we know, the Wild Cards consist of kids. This job could've been done by an adult, since it's a very hard and scary job, but I believe these footsteps belong to the Terror Twins."

"What!" Silvis gasped again. He didn't know why he was so surprised. Of course it was them!

"They must've insisted that they be sent. They want to help Charlie while also doing their job as Wild Cards. Of course, I should've known! This is the first step of the plan! They know we know too much and now the next step is to get rid of us!"

"What?" Silvis said. *Get rid of us? Why would they do that?*

"Silvis, the Wild Cards are very cruel. I doubt they'd kill us, but they could definitely do something horrible to... get rid of us."

Silvis could think of many horrible things they'd do to them and couldn't believe anyone could be that cruel. He shook his head in disbelief. This case was already dangerous enough, and now, Silvis was at the risk of being destroyed, or possibly even killed, depending on what the Wild Cards might do. He now seriously second-guessed ever getting involved in this case. How much trouble had he gotten himself into? He was no fighter, or detective, or someone who could fight a group of deadly kids. Maybe I should say that I quit. *Maybe I should live my normal, boring life in my house.*

"I know what you're thinking, Silvis," Junior said, startling Silvis again and interrupting his thoughts.

"No, you don't," Silvis spat, his anger rising. *Why is Junior acting like he knows what I'm going through? He'll never understand. In fact, it's Junior's fault that I'm in the middle of this case that could kill me.*

"I'm sorry," Junior added. "I know you don't want to be part of this. You can quit if you want, I understand."

But this was his chance to make a difference, whether he solved it or not, whether he was recognized for it or not. I could finally be useful. The words echoed in his mind. His life never had any purpose except to be alive and be happy. His only friend was Polo, who was more of an annoying little brother he had to look after. He never thought he'd make any friends, and now here he was, with friends and a purpose. He had to do the right thing, no matter what.

"No," Silvis said sternly. "I won't leave or give up."

Junior smiled at him and patted his shoulder.

"Tomorrow at five," Silvis told Junior. "Where are we meeting?"

"Newberry Park," Junior said.

At school the next day, Silvis was having a good time watching Charlie sulk. Charlie didn't spread any rumors or try to be the center of attention. Instead, he tried not to get any attention at all, even though everyone tried asking him questions about the detective challenge. (No one got any answers.) To his delight, Silvis even got a few moments to make fun of Charlie, until Charlie threatened to tell a teacher. The Terror Twins were also in bad moods, and they beat up anyone who said anything bad about Charlie. They didn't dare to go near Junior, knowing that he was the center of attention and everyone would yell and probably tell on them.

Soon, the time for Silvis to meet Junior at Newberry Park had come. Silvis got on his bike and rode to the huge, lime green grass field. He figured Junior would be here because this was where they met with Elly, Willow, and Ghost. Silvis spotted Junior under a tree, taking notes on a notepad.

He noticed that Junior was constantly looking behind him and to his left, but he didn't even glance towards the parking lot, where Silvis would obviously come from.

Silvis walked up to him. "Hey Junior."

Junior jumped up and dropped his notebook, then stumbled backwards. He caught himself before he fell. Silvis suppressed a laugh as Junior got up from his weird position that had saved him, muttering, "Oh, sorry," while quickly jotting down some more notes.

Silvis wasn't sure what to say. "Is everything alright?"

"Oh, yeah, um, just looking out for anyone spying or sneaking up on us," Junior replied.

It hadn't occurred to him that someone could definitely be watching them or planning to attack them. "Right," Silvis concluded. "So, where are we going?"

"I believe there is something about to take place at our school. Something illegal." Junior handed Silvis an envelope. Inside of it, the note said:

Come to school at 4 P.M. on Wednesday.
YLO robbery. Sending Morpher. Be there in office.
Chaos coming.

At first, this was very odd to Silvis. "So, who exactly wrote this? Are they okay? Do they need therapy?" Silvis joked.

Junior laughed, "No, they're actually smart."

"Where'd you get this from?" Silvis asked.

"Thought I'd take a look in one of the twins' backpacks. Don't even know which one, they look the same. The message is written weirdly, kind of as a code. If someone other than a wild card found it, it would be bad, so it's written in this weird wording. I have decoded some of it. I don't know what YLO means, but there's a robbery at the school at four. I believe 'Morpher' means a wild card in a morph suit and they're going to be robbing the office. I don't know what they're gonna steal, but we have to prevent this or get some evidence."

They were at the Hillstretch Hills, and they were walking through the empty park. They walked for some time until they heard rustling nearby. They both froze. Junior suddenly took a step back in panic and then whispered, "Run."

Immediately, Silvis sprinted to the right as Junior ran behind him. There were multiple trees in the dense forest-like area, and Silvis just kept running. He heard rustling and footsteps much louder than Junior's from behind him. Silvis risked a glance back, and to his horror, he saw two large figures wearing black hoodies, pitch black masks, and jeans charging towards them. Silvis jerked his head forward and stumbled out of the way of a huge tree. The figures chasing them were definitely the Terror Twins. What Junior had said had come true. *They're here to get rid of us.*

Silvis tried stuffing all the horrifying thoughts into the back of his mind, but they kept coming back. At least they motivated him to keep running. The Terror Twins were much faster than Silvis and Junior, who knew they couldn't outrun them for long. Junior began to slow down, and shortly after, Silvis did, too, trying hard to catch his breath.

He could now see the edge of the forest so clearly; it was right in front of him. He was at the edge of the hill they were on, but he had no idea how far down the drop was. *Will we have to jump?* Out of breath, Silvis stopped at the edge. Tall trees and thorny bushes blocked both sides, and there was nowhere to run. Junior ran to his side a few seconds later, and the Terror Twins stopped a few feet in front of them. Over the edge of the hill was a large lake and a very high drop. There was a neighborhood next to the lake.

Their only option was to jump, but the fall was way too high. Silvis was about to ask if they should jump, but then Junior whispered, "Don't jump. I've got this." Although unsure, Silvis nodded.

"Don't move! Unless you'd rather fall in that river and break a million bones!" one of the twins shouted. "Put your hands in the air!"

Junior put his hands in the air and so did Silvis.

One of the twins pulled out a syringe with green liquid inside. This is how they get rid of us, Silvis thought hopelessly. Whatever is in there can't be good.

This was the end. The twin with the syringe slowly approached Silvis. The other twin also pulled out a syringe and walked towards Junior. "Don't move," Junior whispered to Silvis under his breath.

The twins stood in front of Silvis and Junior. Goodbye, Silvis thought.

"Ready?" one twin asked.

"Ready," said the other. The twin in front of Silvis grabbed his arm and the twin in front of Junior reached for his arm. But he never grabbed ahold of it. Junior stomped on the twin's foot, and the twin let out a shriek of agony. Junior grabbed onto the twin's waist, and the other twin jabbed the syringe towards Silvis's arm, but Silvis ducked right in time.

Silvis realized what Junior was trying to do. He kicked the feet of the twin Junior was holding, causing the twin to lose his balance. Right at that moment, Junior pushed the twin, who plunged off the edge of the hill.

Wham! The twin hit the side of the hill. Splash! He landed in the water. After watching his brother fall, the other twin charged towards Silvis. They wrestled towards the edge of the hill, and Silvis was about to fall off.

Crack! Junior charged into the twin from behind. Silvis let go of the twin, who went toppling over the edge, but Junior grabbed onto Silvis's arm just in time and heaved him up to the top.

"Help!" the twin's voice called. He was hanging onto the edge.

"He's gonna come after us again if we help him," Junior said.

"Then what do we do?" Silvis asked.

"I have an idea." Junior reached into his backpack as the twin struggled helplessly on the edge. Junior quickly whipped out a very long rope and tied one end to the closest tree.

"I can't hold on for much longer!" the twin yelled. Junior grabbed the other end of the rope, ran over to the twin and tied it tightly around his arm.

"Junior, you're brilliant!" Silvis said. He felt like he would've been fine if this twin fell off the edge, too, but he felt good knowing that they could stop him and save him.

"Help should come for you soon." Junior said. He turned to Silvis and said, "C'mon, let's get out of here."

They sprinted towards the woods eagerly as the wind howled into their faces. Once they made it back to Newberry Park, Junior said, "We've had enough for today. We're going to the school tomorrow when the Wild Cards will be there."

"What?" Silvis asked.

"If we can find them and somehow get their masks off, we can take a picture of them. We would have proof and then we could get them arrested. And I'd also have a big advantage in the detective challenge."

Relieved that they had escaped the twins but still feeling bad for the one that fell off, Silvis took a nap and relaxed for the rest of the day. Junior had said that the Wild Cards probably wouldn't immediately send someone to attack them once they found out what had happened to the twins. But when they did send someone, it would be someone much stronger. Polo was also extremely surprised when he heard what happened and, to Silvis's surprise, didn't bother him or do anything bad.

•

The next day, Charlie seemed more hopeful, but he still avoided Silvis and Junior. The Terror Twins didn't come to school, either; Silvis figured that they must be in the hospital after what happened yesterday. Although he wasn't worried, Silvis still kept a close eye on Charlie all day. That hopeful look on him disturbed Silvis for some odd reason; he felt as if Charlie knew something important that no one else knew. Still, Silvis wasn't alarmed by this thought and continued on his day. Silvis and his class took social studies tests, which weren't very hard.

After saying goodbye to Ghost, who seemed to be always writing down notes which he didn't want anyone to see, Silvis walked home with Willow. They talked about school and the case, but not the encounter with the Terror Twins. Although she was someone who was very trustworthy in Silvis's opinion, Silvis still thought that what had happened the day before should stay between himself and Junior for the time being. He didn't want to freak her out, either.

When the turn came and Willow and Silvis parted ways for the rest of the walk, Silvis noticed lots of signs all over the neighborhood. There was a picture of a wild card envelope at the top, and these words beneath it:

IF ANYONE RECEIVED AN ENVELOPE THAT LOOKS LIKE THIS, DO NOT OPEN IT! IT IS DANGEROUS AND IT WILL GET YOU INVOLVED WITH THE Griefings. PLEASE PUT THE ENVELOPE IN THE MAILBOX OUTSIDE OF 467 NEWBURG STREET.

Silvis hadn't thought about collecting wild card invitations, but this was definitely a good idea. He wondered if Junior would collect anything.

A couple hours later, Silvis was back at Newberry Park with Junior. They walked over to the school, this time with no interruptions. Once they made it, Junior pulled out ski masks for both of them. It did look suspicious, but the only people who would see them would be Wild Cards. They crept behind a tree for what felt like half an hour until they finally saw someone approaching the school.

The person, who was wearing a morph suit (which Junior said was probably the Morpher), climbed over the front gate and crept into the school. After him came four others, except these people were wearing black uniforms and the top of a morph suit to cover their faces. One of them had a cast and crutches. Silvis and Junior knew that this was the twin they had pushed off the hill.

After everyone else climbed over the fence, they opened the gate for the twin to come in and then closed it. They headed over to the fence on the other side of the blacktop that led to all the classrooms. Silvis realized one of the figures was much taller and bigger than the rest. They were probably an adult. This fence was much taller, and it was nearly impossible to climb. One of the figures fumbled a lockpick and began trying to pick the lock on the school fence.

"Now is our chance," said Junior.

Stealthily and quietly, Silvis and Junior trudged over to the front gate beside the parking lot. Silvis climbed it first and then Junior did. They walked for a little bit and then hid in the corner behind the fence the Wild Cards were trying to open. Junior snuck a peek for a split second, then whispered in Silvis's ear, "Four of them are watching and guarding. The other is trying to open the lo—"

Click! Silvis almost jumped when the fence creaked open. Once the Wild Cards ran through, Silvis and Junior quietly tiptoed away as fast as they could, then walked into the library, where the door was surprisingly open. There was muttering as the Wild Cards ran to the office. Silvis and Junior were able to watch them through the window as they walked up to the office door and began trying to pick the lock.

"So, what's the plan?" Silvis whispered.

"Now we wait," Junior replied. "When the time comes, you'll make a distraction and I'll sneak into the office while they investigate. I'll take a picture of the kid robbing the office. I don't think we can prevent the robbery."

Click! The office door swung open.

"We can't give them much time. In a minute, you'll make the distraction."

"Okay, what should I do?" Silvis replied.

"Here," Junior said. He unzipped the heavy backpack he was carrying and took out a big, red button.

"What's that?"

"It's a toy. When you click the button, it will make a creaking noise. It's used for pranks, but we can make use of it."

Silvis nodded and accepted the red button from Junior. The bright red colors would stand out in the evening sky, so Silvis tucked it in his pocket.

"One more thing," Junior said. "After you press it, wait a few seconds and press it again so they know where it's coming from. Also, you should probably press it outside of an unlocked door, then open it."

"But Junior," Silvis protested.

"What?"

"Are you sure you can handle it alone in there? I should come too, just in case."

"Fine, you're right. Set off the distraction and go into the office after."

"Alright."

Silvis tiptoed out of the library from the back door, and he tested a few door handles until he found an unlocked one. Silvis fished the red button out of his pocket and clicked it. *Creak!* A moment later, he heard a bunch of whispering.

Carefully but quickly, Silvis pulled open the door without making a sound and put down the door stopper. Silvis heard footsteps pounding all around him as people searched for the noise. After about twenty seconds, the Wild Cards were close, but they still hadn't found the door. Their footsteps were a few corners away. He pressed the button again, and their footsteps rushed towards him. He quickly scrambled away as the Wild Cards' footsteps got closer.

Silvis was walking around the library to head to the office, clutching the button tightly in his hand, when a voice whispered, "Silvis!"

Suddenly, footsteps came their way, and Junior pulled Silvis into the library. They hid behind a bookshelf and Silvis whispered, "Junior! What are you doing here?! You should be in the office!"

"They left someone behind to guard the door. I needed your button to distract the one guarding. Then you came."

Footsteps thudded across the library as a wild card searched for Silvis and Junior. "Come out!" he called. "You're already done for!"

Junior risked a peek and whispered, "He's on the other side!"

Junior crouched and headed towards the exit. Silvis followed. The wild card, who was determined Silvis and Junior were on the other side, kept taunting them and telling them to reveal themselves. Silvis and Junior slipped out of the library and headed straight for the office. The door was wide open, and Junior snuck inside. Silvis followed carefully and quietly.

Silvis lay low and followed Junior; the office was huge, there were many desks for staff, each desk with many items and decorations. They heard whispering from close by. Silvis couldn't make out much, but he heard, "Take off your masks."

Junior must've heard this too, because he hastily quickened his pace. They saw the two tall figures and the even bigger figure who seemed like an adult. Junior pulled his camera out of his backpack and began recording. The figures were on the other side of the hall. The two tall figures were obviously the Terror Twins. The one with the crutches said, "Yes," and removed his mask. Silvis felt an ache of guilt when he saw his face.

The crutches. We did that to him. I did that to him, Silvis thought.

Although they were at the other end of the hall and beside a desk, Junior still didn't want to risk being caught, so he placed the camera down at the edge of the desk and shuffled over behind the desk. They could still see the camera, and it wasn't likely that the Wild Cards would notice it.

The other twin took off his mask and the adult-looking person said, "Good." The adult-looking person took off his own mask, and under it was another mask.

A mask with X's on the spot where your eyes would see through.

Silvis held back a gasp. That had to be Ghast, based on how Junior had explained him. Silvis's fear was replaced with disappointment when he realized that Ghast wasn't going to take off his other mask.

"So, boys. Let's make this simple. You have failed me and the Master," Ghast said. "And because of your foolishness, I am now in trouble for your stupid actions."

"Sir, we can—" the twin without the crutches began, but he was cut off by Ghast intervening.

"There is no need for an explanation, Meryl. That boy is no detective. He walked right into my hut in the paintball field. He narrowly escaped. If the Master hadn't said not to kill anyone, I would've murdered him on the spot. And yet, you failed to stop that fool and his friend, and you managed to also get pushed off a cliff. At least for now, we've got one of you to use. Those guys were idiots not to push you both off, it would've helped them a ton. And it would've saved me from your annoyingness."

"Sir, you underestimate them. Of course, we are much stronger than them. But it was a simple mistake. It won't ever happen again, sir," the twin named Meryl said. "And once Dex is healed, he won't fall off again."

"That better happen," Ghast spat. "You fools are more useless than that kindergarten distraction we have. But of course, we have to follow Master's plans." There was irritation in his voice. Silvis guessed that he was probably fighting the urge to say that all of the Master's plans were horrible. "Now, once Morpher pulls off the robbery, you're gonna follow the next phase properly. Now, go find that Morpher guy."

The twins walked around the corner of the hall and Junior ended the recording.

"This is great," Junior said. "We have all the proof we need."

"Now we gotta try and stop the Morpher," said Silvis.

"I wouldn't do that if I were you," a cold voice snarled. Silvis almost leapt in fright but quickly caught himself. He turned around to see the Morpher standing in front of them. Silvis was about to run for his life. He had to.

"Don't move, or I'll call the others," the Morpher threatened. Silvis stopped himself from running.

"How long have you been here?" Junior asked.

"The whole time," the Morpher replied.

"What? You didn't stop us?" Silvis asked, confused.

"The Master would be much more proud if I stopped you guys from getting the whole recording rather than a portion of it."

"Smart," Junior complimented him.

"Give me the camera and this won't be hard."

"Never," Silvis replied, without thinking. He had committed to solving this case, and he wasn't going to give up.

Junior glanced back at him with a surprised look.

"Oh, boy. I wish I didn't have to do this. You sure are a stubborn one." Silvis had forgotten that he was still clutching the red button in his right hand, but Junior grabbed the button from Silvis's hand and chucked it straight at the Morpher's face. The Morpher hardly had a moment to react.

Clunk! Clunk! The button hit his face and hit the ground. The Morpher let out a screech of pain as Silvis and Junior bolted away.

They ran out of the office as the Wild Cards' footsteps thundered towards them. They ran around the library and bolted for the gate. Soon, a few Wild Cards were on their tails, running after them as they ran through the fence. They ran across the blacktop and headed towards the front gates. Silvis couldn't keep running for long, and he was struggling to catch his breath. The Wild Cards were gaining on them. They weren't going to make it. *Unless...* an idea burst into Silvis's head.

"The backpack!" Silvis shouted.

Junior got his message and shortly after realized that it was a good idea. "Head for the playground," Junior said.

A moment later, Junior took a sharp turn to the left and sprinted towards the playground. Silvis ran after him. The Wild Cards were confused by this, and they stopped for a moment before running after them. The playground was a large, light blue play area. It consisted of three different big structures with slides and obstacles. There was also a zipline and five different sets of swings. Junior ran up the largest structure, which was the main one. Part of the zipline was connected to this structure. They had a few moments before the Wild Cards would catch up to them.

Junior quickly unzipped the backpack and searched through it frantically. "There's nothing useful in here!" he complained. "I don't even have the rope!" Then out of nowhere, Junior's desperate voice turned into a hopeful one. "Aha!" he cheered quietly as he pulled out a water bottle.

"A water bottle? What's that gonna do?" Silvis questioned.

"Make them trip."

The Wild Cards charged up the stairs of the playground. Silvis ran to his favorite place on the playground: the zipline. He saw Junior run to the wobbly wooden bridge on his right that led to the second structure. Silvis ran across the playground to the zipline and stepped on the round platform. He held onto the long line. Behind him, Junior was dumping water onto the bridge and three Wild Cards sprinting towards the zipline. Two Wild Cards ran over to the bridge and slipped on the large puddle of water. He knew Junior was going to escape, but he had to act now if he wanted to escape.

Silvis quickly launched himself off the playground and the zipline began moving to the stop at the Zipline Station, a tower-like structure where all the ziplines were. There were two structures, and Silvis, to his luck, was going towards the one closest to the blacktop. The three Wild Cards had climbed off the largest play structure and were running towards the Zipline Station. But they weren't fast enough, and Silvis had a head start.

When the zipline was close enough to the tower, Silvis jumped off the platform and grabbed onto one of the playground ladders that led up to the Zipline Station. He climbed down the ladder, and when he was close enough to the ground, he jumped off. He could now see Junior, who had just made it to the blacktop and was sprinting towards the gates. Silvis ran across the tanbark and onto the blacktop.

The three Wild Cards were now behind Silvis but still quite far away. Silvis kept running, and soon, Junior had climbed over the gates. Silvis started climbing the gates, the Wild Cards getting closer and closer. As he was about to climb over the top, a heavy, large hand with an extremely strong grip seized his foot.

"Argh!" Silvis yelled, and the inescapable grip pulled him. It was Ghast.

"Give up, boy!" Ghast's menacing voice roared. Silvis couldn't fight the grip for much longer, and the other Wild Cards were now catching up. Silvis kicked his feet. Ghast struggled and dodged Silvis's kicks.

Finally, Silvis hit Ghast's face. Thud! Ghast roared in pain, letting go of Silvis's foot. Silvis climbed over the gates, where Junior waiting for him. He was about to jump down when Junior whispered, "Don't jump!" Junior pointed to a puddle of water that he'd poured.

Silvis climbed down, avoiding the puddle. Ghast was now climbing the gates. But Silvis and Junior sprinted away into the forest, across the road they had come from.

"I think we lost him!" said Silvis gleefully. "He won't be able to find us in here."

"That was close," said Junior. "We found out so much information."

"And I'm exhausted. Let's talk about it tomorrow." said Silvis.

•

Silvis woke up with a painful headache. He had a dream about a violin locked up somewhere in his basement, but it didn't feel like a dream. It felt like a message. He had also seen this same violin being burned in flames, but he was never able to get a good view of it. He was having trouble sleeping, as well, ever since they had almost been caught by Wild Cards four days ago. Junior was still getting a bunch of envelopes which were supposed to be wild card invitations. He was planning to do it after the weekend was over, giving people plenty of time to send in their possible wild card invitations.

The detective challenge choosing day was today. Silvis was sure they would win. They had so many clues and, better yet, proof of the Terror Twins being Wild Cards.

Now, most of the fourth- and fifth-graders were gathered in the crowd. Everyone fell silent as Charlie approached Junior.

"Hello, Charlie. As you know, this is the deciding day, where the winner of the detective challenge will be chosen."

Charlie had a smirk on his face, and he looked like he knew he was going to win. This worried Silvis, even though he knew Charlie would never be able to find any clues.

"Let's get straight into it. You may go first," Junior said.

Charlie's evil smirk grew wider and he spoke. "I have found a lot of things, far more than this fool could ever find. Firstly, the girl named Willow is a 'wild card,' as Junior calls them. Wild Cards are the ones who caused the Griefings.

And Willow is one of them. I have proof here." He pulled out a sticky note. "It says, 'We will raid the school in two weeks. Everyone must be there. No one in the school shall live. I'll be thinking about the plan at Newberry Park at 7:00. -Willow.'"

"You don't know that's hers!" Silvis shouted, angry that Charlie was framing Willow.

Charlie showed the note to a few people from Silvis's class in the front row. "Is this Willow's handwriting?"

Everyone in Silvis's class knew how Willow's handwriting looked because the teacher always used her writing as an example. The people who saw the note gasped and moved away from Willow. "It's hers!" someone shouted.

Silvis saw Willow, looking terrified, make eye contact with Junior, and Junior mouthed "I've got this."

Charlie folded the note and put it in his pocket. "So, me and the twins went to Newberry Park and we confronted Willow. She confessed that she was the right-hand man of the person who created the Griefings! But then a bunch of Wild Cards jumped out of nowhere and rescued her! The twins and I fought them, and the twins almost beat them, but there were too many and they got away. So there, Junior. I think we have a clear winner here." He stuck his tongue out and smirked.

Everyone in the crowd was astonished by what Charlie had said and definitely believed him. Silvis was unsure whether they would win after all. Was Willow a traitor?

"Actually," Junior began. "What I have found out proves everything Charlie just said wrong. Now. Silvis and I were searching for clues near the school. That's when we found this video." Junior pulled out the camera they used to record the twins from his backpack. He projected the recording onto a screen behind him and everyone watched.

Suddenly, Charlie's smirk turned into a horrified look. There was no audio to the recording. Junior must've disabled it because there was a lot of key information in the audio.

"The man in the video is the same man who drugged two boys during the Griefings, and he is, of course, a wild card. And so, the Terror Twins were here in the school office with him, wearing the same costumes. That isn't any coincidence, is it?"

Now everyone was staring at the Twins, afraid that they might suddenly kill someone.

"You—little—" Meryl bellowed in deep hatred.

"We'll kill you! He's lying, guys! This is—is some sort of s-set up!" Dex roared. But the crowd didn't buy any of this, and people yelled out swears and denial.

Junior wasn't at all afraid of this threat. "So," he continued, "I don't think we should believe a word Charlie said. The part where he said the twins helped him fight the Wild Cards is just hilarious!" Junior laughed loudly, and others began to talk and laugh. The twins looked like they were about to explode. A few moments later, sirens cried out in the distance.

"What? Police? Coming here?" Dex snapped.

Silvis was also unsure why they were here. Had they found out that the Wild Cards robbed the office? Silvis noticed Junior grinning as the police parked outside the gates. *He is happy about the police coming, but why?* Silvis questioned himself.

A yard duty ran over to the gates and pushed them open. "What seems to be the problem?" the yard duty asked. There were two tall officers who walked onto the blacktop and whispered something to the yard duty. They then noticed the huge crowd and walked up to them.

"Hello, kids. We're looking for two twins named Dex and—" The officer who was talking was cut off by the twins bolting away.

"That's them!" Junior shouted.

The officers ran after the twins and Junior yelled to the crowd, "The criminals are getting away, come on!" And he ran off.
Silvis ran after him, and half of the crowd did, too. The twins were close to the front gates, but they weren't fast enough for the officers. The officers pushed the twins onto the ground and cuffed them.

"Are you the one that called?" one of the officers asked Junior.

"Yes," he replied.

"Tell us everything you know."

Junior told the officers everything he had just told the crowd, and he also told them about the twins attacking him and Silvis. After that, the cops took the twins away in their police car and drove off.

"Now, let's get this challenge over with," Junior said, sighing.

Junior led the crowd back to where they were before. He took a piece of paper out of his backpack. "Charlie, write the words 'Detective Charlie's voting ballot' on this paper." He handed Charlie a pencil and the paper. Charlie wrote it down miserably. "Charlie, can you hand me the note you claim Willow wrote?"

Silvis was surprised that Charlie didn't argue, but he looked like he wanted to die and simply handed Junior the note. "Thank you," Junior said. He held up the note and the piece of paper Charlie wrote on for the kids in the front row.

"As you can see here, the handwriting looks the exact same. So, Charlie here wrote that note and pretended Willow wrote it." The crowd was impressed, and they all started whispering loudly. Willow looked relieved, and Silvis was overjoyed.

"So... Who is the detective of Hillstretch?" The crowd burst into applause and cheers. "Wasn't it always obvious?" Junior beamed.

CHAPTER 8

SEARCHING

Silvis's head seared with pain when he got up. He had been taking care of Polo and cleaning his house all day since he had come back from school, and yet, the dream about a burning violin in his basement wouldn't go away. It felt so real, Silvis wasn't sure if it was a dream or a memory. *Maybe there is a violin in my basement,* he thought. He decided he was going to check.

Silvis could hear Polo making dinner. He slowly walked down the stairs, trying his best not to step on any creaky stairs because once Polo knew he was awake, it would be chaos. Silvis knew if others saw his basement, they would be terrified. It was the type of old, abandoned basement that would be in a horror movie. But he was never scared of it, even the first time he went in it.

Silvis slowly opened the old basement door and began his half-hour search of the entire basement. He looked in every closet and on every shelf. He searched every rooms and even an abandoned bathroom with a nest of spiders. Lastly, he looked through what looked like endless cabinets filling the hall.

In the last cabinet he opened, he saw a very old-looking scroll. He picked it up and took a good look at it. He didn't want to open the scroll because it looked very dusty and old, and there was obviously no violin in there. Frustrated, Silvis jammed the scroll back onto the shelf. He was determined to find something to end his endless nightmares about this violin, but there was nothing there. That was his last hope. It must have been a dream, after all.

CLANG!

A shiny object fell out of the scroll onto the ground: a shiny, gold key. It Silvis picked it up. *What does this lead to?* He felt his heart thumping. He immediately raced around the basement, feeling around on the walls and floor for a secret door. *This has to unlock something!*

Finally, Silvis found a sealed trapdoor! He pushed the key through the sealed surface and into the keyhole.

What is down there? Will the key even open the trapdoor? He stopped himself from thinking of the possibilities and twisted the key.

Click! Silvis knew the key had worked. But the door was still sealed. He needed to break the seal. He ran over to the other side of the basement and grabbed an old knife he saw lying on a wooden counter. He used this knife to cut the seal around the trapdoor. After he was done, he put back the knife and opened the trapdoor.

A whiff of dust assaulted Silvis's face, but he brushed it off easily. He was surprised that the secret room didn't smell bad at all. Without thinking any further, he stepped into the dark room. There was plenty of dust in the room, but that didn't stop Silvis. Eventually, he found the light switch and flipped it. The light bulb worked just fine and looked a couple years old. The room wasn't very big and it looked just like the basement.

But in the corner of the room, something caught his eye. Something stuck out from the top of a table covered with a long, silver tapestry. This was the only thing in the room. Silvis realized that he remembered this tapestry from his dream. He rushed over to it and took a good look. There was definitely something on top of the table, under the tapestry. Hastily, he pulled off the tapestry.

Silvis almost tripped over in surprise. There, in front of him on the table, was a silver violin case. It looked like real silver, definitely very valuable. This had to be the violin from his dreams!

Carefully, Silvis opened the two locks on the case. He knew how to play the violin very well, and everyone said he was a master at it. He had been taught by his mother starting when he was two. His mom was probably the best violin teacher ever, but for some reason, he could never remember how his mom's violin looked. He wondered if there was even a violin in the case. From his dream, he only remembered a gray violin and something blue.

He opened the case. This time, he did fall over.

He could hardly think. There was no way that what he had seen was really there. He got up and looked again. In front of him was a silver violin with light blue strings. On the back of the scroll, there was a swirl of dark blue.

It was the legendary Sapphire Mando: the world's best violin.

The violin was coated with diamond dust and the strings were made of one of the world's best sapphires. On the scroll of the violin was the same type of sapphire, a darker blue color. The violin was surprisingly not shiny at all. The famous bow, which the violin was always played with, had some of the best horsehair in the world, and the stick was dark brown and extremely sturdy.

The Sapphire Mando was named after the famous violinist and violin maker, Goliath Mando, and its sapphire strings. This violin was priceless.

I shouldn't touch this. I shouldn't have this. Should I give it to the authorities? But it's in my house—

Silvis's arguing thoughts halted. He saw something on the violin. Under the strings and behind the bridge, words were carved onto the violin. Silvis leaned closer and read the words. "Silvis Wren." This was the same spot where Goliath's name originally was, before it was passed down to his son. *Why is my name there?*

"No way!" he blurted.

He could feel his finger shaking, but he touched his name. He felt something powdery. *How can the diamond dust come off?* There were words on the spot that had the diamond dust, above his name: "Whitney Wren."

"That's my mother!" Silvis said to himself. "My mother used to own the Sapphire Mando!"

Silvis noticed the pouch in the case where the rosin was supposed to be. On the pouch were the words, "Diamond dust in here if you need to cover up names." Silvis wasn't sure how or why his mother once owned the Sapphire Mando or why his name was carved on it, but this violin had always been his motivation and his dream had been to see it.

Now that dream was true. And even if it belonged to him, he still had to treat it with respect. Silvis opened the pouch and took out a jar of diamond dust. He poured just enough on top of his mother's name, and after a few seconds, he scooped the dust off the top and put it back in the jar. Just like magic, the dust had worked perfectly and had completely covered his mother's name.

Silvis decided since it was his, he was going to play it. But he couldn't let Polo notice him, so he had to sneak into the backyard.

He put the violin back into the case and slowly walked out of the basement.

He managed to close the old door without making a lot of noise, and then he snuck towards the backyard door in the living room. Fortunately for Silvis, Polo was no longer in the kitchen cooking and Silvis was able to slide open the door and go outside.

Should I tell Junior about this? I probably shouldn't, at least for now. We already have a case to deal with and this would get in the way.

Silvis put the shoulder rest (also in the case) into position. He put the bow to the tip of the E string. *I shouldn't be playing this. It's a legendary violin and I'm just a boy. I shouldn't even be holding anything nearly this important and awesome.* But he fought away the bad thoughts and took a deep breath.

Silvis played a beautiful song his mother had taught him when he was young. It was already a beautiful song, but on the Sapphire Mando, it sounded even more beautiful. Silvis fell into a trance and kept playing. He couldn't fathom how wonderful it sounded.

After Silvis finished, he noticed something. The royal blue sapphire on the violin's scroll was glowing. *Does this mean I'm playing well? Is there a special feature built into the sapphire?* He began to play another song. A moment later, Silvis heard a weird noise that sounded like something sizzling.

BOOM!

A jet of what appeared to be blue-colored wind blasted towards a large pine tree and made a hole straight through it. This came from the scroll of the violin.

"What the—the sapphire did that!" Silvis realized. *Was that really blue wind?* His mouth dropped open as he stared at the hole going straight through the large trunk of the tree. So there was a secret in this violin. Silvis looked at the sapphire on the scroll, which was now slowly losing the glow. *It's almost like it charged up,* he thought.

As confused as he was, Silvis decided to drop the topic and put away the violin. He didn't want to get hurt. He was about to put it back in the case when there was a ruffling noise from behind him. *Oh no.*

Polo sprinted towards him. "What's that?" Polo asked. "Is that a violin? When did you get a violin?" He stared dreamily at the case and then suddenly jumped back. Polo spelled out the words "Sapphire Mando" in sign language.

"What?" Silvis gasped. "How do you—I mean—"

"I know what it is," Polo replied.

"Listen here, Polo, you must not say anything about this. Do not touch it either, please. I don't know why it was in the basement, but it just was." Polo stared at the hole in the large tree trunk.

"This thing is weird and dangerous. I'm not gonna touch it, and you have to promise me that you won't, either. Pinky promise?" said Silvis.

"I know," Polo replied. "It is super important."

He felt like he could now trust Polo, so he slowly placed the case onto the ground. Polo walked over to Silvis and held out his pinky. He stared into the little monkey's eyes. He entwined his finger with Polo's. With his other hand, Polo said, "I swear." Silvis held back a gasp. He could feel goosebumps.

When Silvis was a kid, he always made pinky promises with his mother. He didn't remember her much, but he knew pinky promises were a thing that his family did. But when there were flames in Silvis's house and before his parents disappeared, Silvis remembered his mom telling him that he had to take care of Polo no matter what.

"Our family has a tradition," she had explained. "We call it the pinky swear. When you make a pinky promise and say, 'I swear,' it is the most important promise ever, and you must never break it. We rarely use this promise, but now you must promise me that you shall take care of Polo at all costs."

She had held out her pinky and Silvis had wrapped his around hers. "Now, say you swear," she had told him.

"I swear," he had said.

Then she had told him to tell Polo what he had committed to and make the pinky swear. That was exactly what he did. Since that day, he always knew it was important. And now Polo had used it.

Silvis knew that Polo was going to keep this promise no matter what. "Why would you—how—" Silvis stuttered. He had no idea what to say.

"I don't know how or why, but I can tell this is important," Polo answered. Silvis was way too shocked to say anything, and he decided to put away the violin and not question Polo.

•

Two days later, Silvis biked to school and tried clearing out all thoughts of the Sapphire Mando from his head. It didn't work. How could he stop thinking about it?

At morning recess, Silvis spotted Ghost over by the benches, not taking notes or busy at all.

"Hey, Ghost!" Silvis called.

"Hey, Silvis!" Ghost replied. "So,...case coming along well?"

"Yeah," Silvis answered.

"Junior did great in the challenge. I assume you helped him?"

"Yes, I did."

"Well, it would be a pleasure for me to help you guys, I haven't really been much help, but I'm great at fighting. And I'm sure you guys will be in some situations when you'll need my help. You definitely needed me when that SUV was trying to kill you."

"Yep. Well, it would be great for you to help us. I don't know when we'll search for more clues, but I'll let you know." Silvis was tempted to tell Ghost about his meeting with Junior where they planned to look at the wild card invitations Junior was sent, but he decided to keep it between him and Junior.

Junior was definitely the school's hero, while Charlie was trying not to be noticed. People laughed at him, teased him, and whispered when they saw him. However, Willow was the most furious. Although she was happy that she wasn't Charlie's victim, she was outraged at Charlie for making up everything and making her the main enemy.

A rumor was spreading across fifth grade that Willow had beaten up Charlie during recess, and Silvis was pretty sure it was true, because he had seen Charlie entering the office with a bloody nose. He was crying so loud that kids on the grass field could hear him.

All the kids were also wondering what happened to the Terror Twins. Their arrest was on the news, but the police didn't reveal who really caught them. There was going to be a trial, and if the twins lost, they'd be in juvenile. Silvis knew there were endless reasons why the police didn't say that Junior caught the twins, some that made sense, some that were reasonable, and some that were unfair and stupid.

Later that day, Silvis dissected a frog for the monthly science test. In total, all of the monthly tests were fifty percent of his science grade. This put a lot of pressure on Silvis, although he had tons of fun doing this experiment.

After that, Silvis's class began a new module in math, which was easy because it was the first lesson of the module. The rest of class passed on, and finally school ended after a few hours. Silvis was super excited because now was the time when he would meet Junior and look at the Wild Card invitations.

•

Ding dong!

Footsteps rushed down the stairs and to the door. "Hello?" Junior asked as he swung the door open. "Oh, Silvis, it's you. Come on in!"

Silvis stepped into Junior's house. He slipped off his shoes and walked into the house. He looked around and saw the familiar walls and living room.

"I'll go get the invitations!" Junior called as he rushed up the stairs.

A moment later, Junior carried a heavy box down the stairs and into the living room. He dumped out the contents of the box onto the carpet. About thirty different letters lay on the ground.

"Wow," Silvis said. "That's a ton!" *How many letters are there? Surely, we'll learn something important—no, not something, tons of important things from all these letters!*

"Yeah, there's a lot," Junior said.

"There's so many—" Silvis began to say.

"Don't get your hopes up. None of them have that word that describes the person on it, and there are so many envelopes that look exactly the same as the wild card one. Most of these are probably just trolls and fakes. It's easy to find the same type of envelope," Junior informed him.

"Oh." Silvis's hope was now washed away. Are there any real invitations in the pile?

Immediately, Junior began opening a message that was right in front of him. Silvis sat next to him, eagerly waiting to see what was in the envelope. Junior pulled it open and took out a note from the envelope.

You're wasting your time! Stop telling people lies, you idiot!
—Charlie

Silvis was surprised that the message was from Charlie. "He wouldn't be so confident and rude now!" Silvis spat. Junior laughed and crumpled the note up and threw it aside. The next message was from the twins, who had misspelled multiple words:

You are stuped and dumb. Give up idot you will never be sucsisful.
Stay out off our way or you will be distoryed.
From the Terror Twins

Silvis and Junior got a good laugh from it and then moved on to the next ones. They were troll letters, too, just like the ones from Charlie or the Terror Twins. There was a totally fake wild card invitation that looked like Verse's, except it was messy and handwritten.

Reading the letters wasn't turning out to be anything like he'd imagined it would be. Junior was counting the letters, and after about ten minutes, they were on their twenty-sixth letter. That meant they only had four more to go. Junior opened the twenty-sixth letter and inside were two notes. "Two?" Junior questioned. "That's new." He picked up one letter that was clearly a letter, not an invitation or any special Wild Card message.

Hello. My name is Kiera and I am in fourth grade. I think I have one of the letters that you said are dangerous and I feel like I can trust you. It is very odd and I am scared. I definitely don't want to be helping the people who caused the Griefings and I hope you can help me. Please meet me at Newberry Park at 5 on Monday and tell me what is going on. I'll be waiting and I hope you come. The other paper has the note I was sent.

From Kiera

Silvis's spirit lifted after he read the letter. None of the other envelopes said anything like this.

"There's no way she's lying! That sounds so real!" Silvis said.

"Don't get your hopes up too high, you can't always trust everyone," Junior said. He eagerly pulled the second paper out of the envelope. It looked like it was definitely a Wild Card letter.

Dear Kiera,

You can call us the YLO. We are a group trying to change this city into a better place and end an important war that has been being fought in the shadows for over two centuries. We need your help, Kiera. Everyone in this city thinks that the Griefings are a bad thing. Our group caused them, and they really aren't a bad thing. You see, it was a distraction so that we could plan something else that's bigger and not harmful at all, although the city would not like it. We know how smart and passionate you are, and we need your help in order to fulfil our plan and reach our goal. There are foes in this town which you must not listen to, but the worst one is a kid detective named Junior. He is working against our group and trying to put us in prison when we have never done anything bad. Trust me, Kiera, we are only trying to help you and this city. Ew evah a terces nopaew taht lliw pleh su. Ew deen uoy ot pleh su ekam ruo txen evom. Ereht si a rettel deirub ni tnorf fo eht noitauc ngis ta dnocces etag ta yrrebwen krap. I know you can decode this message.

From the leader of the YLO

"Well, I guess they're not putting crime at the start of the letter," Junior joked. "I'm glad this girl trusts me enough to give us this note."

"Such a weird note... Junior, do you have any idea what it means?" Silvis asked.

"I'll figure it out." Junior grabbed the note and walked away, his face buried in the letter, studying it like a hawk.

What does this mean? Silvis thought. *What does YLO mean?*

A few minutes later, Junior returned. "I've figured it out," he said. "It's basically the message, but backwards. Decoded, it says, 'We have a secret weapon that will help us. We need you to help us make our next move. There is a letter buried in the front of the caution sign at the second gate at Newberry Park.'"

"She's meeting us at Newberry Park!" Silvis said. "We can find the letter while we're there!"

"Exactly. But we gotta still be careful. Anything can happen," said Junior.

•

A few hours later, Junior had a backpack with a shovel inside and a few other tools. Junior rode to the park on his Segway and Silvis rode his bike. Once they arrived, they looked around for the girl. They walked onto the shiny, lime green grass. They spotted a girl with long, blond hair sitting in the center of the field, reading a book.

"Hey!" Junior called to her.

Her head sprang up. For a moment, she looked at them like they were a threat, then adjusted to a normal expression. "Hi! Are you the one who got my letter?" she asked.

"Yeah, that's me. This is my friend, he's helping me, so I brought him along."

Kiera stared at Silvis for a moment, then looked away.

"Did you decode the message in the letter?" Junior asked.

"Yeah, I did. I'm guessing you did too?"

"Yeah."

"I don't get it, though. Can you explain to me what this all means?"

To Silvis's surprise, Junior hesitated for a moment, then said, "I'll tell you everything in a moment. First, I think we should find the letter at the caution sign!"

"Oh—alright," said Kiera.

Silvis gave Junior a confused look and then they walked off to the caution sign. Kiera ran ahead of them because she knew how to get there. It was like she had it memorized. While she was ahead of them, Silvis heard her muttering. *She's the type of person who talks to herself,* Silvis thought.

Soon, they arrived at the caution sign. There was a lot of moist mud around it. This caution sign had been here for years, and no one had gone past it. There was a rumor that there was a large ditch behind the sign and a kid fell in it. Regardless of what lay ahead of them, they had to start digging.

Junior pulled out his backpack and took out two shovels. He handed one to Silvis and kept one for himself. "Sorry, forgot to bring one for you," Junior said.

"Oh—um—it's okay," Kiera replied.

Silvis and Junior began digging. It was easy to dig because the soil was muddy and wet. Silvis and Junior dug through the soil while Kiera watched them with an uneasy look. *Is she worried about something? Does she know something we don't?* Silvis wasn't sure what the deal with her was. Kiera was a very odd girl.

After digging for about five minutes, Silvis got very tired, and his arms began to give in. Junior kept digging. He must've been super tired but determined.

"Are you sure we should keep digging?" Silvis asked.

"Yeah. We have to find that letter," Junior replied drowsily.

"But what if it isn't really there? Or what if the Wild Cards took it out?" Silvis said.

"I'll just—I found it!"

"What! Where?" Kiera questioned.

Junior reached his hand into the big hole that he and Silvis had created and pulled out something wrapped in wrapping paper. Kiera stepped directly behind Junior. Junior hastily reached for the strings that tied the wrapping paper, but then abruptly stopped.

"Hey, Kiera," Junior called.

"Yeah?" Kiera replied.

"What's my name?"

"Uh, Junior. I mean—"

What? Silvis thought. *How does she know his name?*

"Run!" Junior hollered. Immediately, they both sprinted away, and Kiera ran after them. There was rustling from nearby bushes, and a swarm of seven Wild Cards charged towards Silvis and Junior.

"What?! Junior, what's going on?" Silvis asked while sprinting away.

"It was a setup. I knew it!"

"A setup? How?"

"I'll tell you later, right now we have to keep running!"

Silvis shut his mouth. He hated being in chases. "We won't make it! Into the bushes!" he said.

Silvis, who was a little ahead of Junior, sprinted towards the bushes. Once he was at the bushes, he ran past them (and got poked by a couple of thorns) and entered the woods that surrounded Newberry Park.

Silvis heard Junior entering the woods behind him, filled with many shrubs and bushes to hide behind. He knew the Wild Cards would be in the woods in just a moment. "We have to hide," he said, "or we won't make it."

Silvis ran deeper into the woods until he found a large bush that he could hide behind. He didn't know where Junior was hiding, but all he could do was hope that Junior was safe. Silvis crouched behind a large bush that looked like it was ten feet tall.

Silvis heard rustling as the Wild Cards entered the woods. They were sprinting around, desperate to find Silvis and Junior. Silvis waited, but there was an urge in him to run away, for some reason. His heart was thumping so fast that he felt like he had just run a marathon.

After a few minutes, the footsteps of the Wild Cards got closer to him. *You're not gonna make it. You and Junior are gonna be captured and killed,* a voice in Silvis's head kept saying. The footsteps were now all around him. Through a small gap between the leaves, he could see a Wild Card approaching his bush to inspect it.

The Wild Card turned to check behind the bush and Silvis quickly did what first came to his mind. He grabbed a heavy stick from the ground and threw it behind him as far as could. The stick soared far away and landed on the ground with a loud thud. The Wild Cards all looked up and ran towards the noise. Silvis moved to the side of the bush as they ran and then the front. After a minute, they were far away deep, in the woods. He finally relaxed to catch his breath.

A voice said, "Psst!"

Silvis jumped and almost ran away, but then he saw Junior's head sticking out from behind a tree.

"Junior! You almost gave me a heart attack!" Silvis said.

"Shh. Keep your voice down!" Junior whispered. "We gotta get out of here."

CHAPTER 9

BASE RAID

Silvis and Junior arrived at Junior's house ten minutes later.

"So, how did you know?" Silvis asked.

"It all added up. The odd way she was acting, when she looked at us like enemies, when she was muttering and all that."

"Oh. She was really a Wild Card all along? It seemed like she was trying to help us. I wasn't expecting her to try to kill us."

Junior sighed and opened the door. They both stepped into the house.

"Before we do anything, I'd better check if there's actually a letter in here," Junior announced. He untied the strings and pulled out a piece of paper from the wrapping paper:

How's the kick in the head feel?

Silvis laughed loudly.

"So that's why she was standing behind me," said Junior.

"What should I do?" Silvis asked. "Should I go home now? Do you think they're still looking for us?"

"Hmm. Something has come to my mind. I think we should look at the last three letters in the box."

The first letter Junior opened was from their teacher, Mrs. Coral. It said that Junior should stop this since there already was a detective at the school (which made Silvis laugh) and that they should inform the principal if they knew something. Junior threw away the letter and moved on to the next one.

The next letter was completely blank, but just in case it really said something, Junior took an invisible ink pen and flashed the light across the paper. Sure enough, there was a message. Silvis's cheeks went red when he read it:

If you find this, get trolled

Junior rolled his eyes and then froze.

"What?" Silvis asked.

"There's only one more left!" Junior said. "Hopefully it has something." He tore open the envelope and two papers slid out of it.

Two papers! Silvis thought. *This could be it!* One of the papers was an ordinary letter, but the other was definitely a Wild Card invitation. Junior decided to read the note first.

Right now, I don't have much time, but I noticed your sign. You are probably the only one who knows about the YLO and their messages, so you probably are my last hope. Whoever you are, I know where the YLO's current primary base is. It is an orphan named Kiera's foster parents' abandoned house. Here is the address: 4478 Newbell Court. I have been there before, after I saw the YLO having a meeting at one of the Hillstretch Hills. They captured me and locked me up and put me in a prison in the attic, where a few other kids are imprisoned too. I was able to escape. They are searching for me right now, and I know they'll catch up to me any minute and take me back to the prison. Please rescue me, or I may be in the attic forever. I have also put a letter of the YLO's plans that was sent to some sort of high-ranked person. I hope that you'll find me and figure out who is behind the sinister group.

- Felix Westrough

"Oh no," Silvis whispered softly.

"There's no way this guy is telling the truth, it's all just another setup!" Junior growled.

"Are you sure, though? What if he really is in trouble?" Silvis asked.

"Doubtful. A small chance isn't worth risking our butts."

Silvis could tell that Junior didn't want to believe that this person was telling the truth. He must've been tired from what happened, and so was Silvis. Junior snatched up the second paper, which was a Wild Card invitation.

To Ghast,

I am grateful for how much of a help you have been to our group, General. This project shall be successful and most definitely won't fail. The secret weapon is too much of a risk, for it has been forgotten for over two centuries. We will only use it when necessary, in the end, of course. And do not ever let any of my messages fall into the wrong hands. I know you already lost one.

The next stage of the project will be starting soon. No killing is involved yet, but now things must be more harsh. While the city is completely clueless about what is going on, this plan is being greatly executed in the shadows. I know I said no killing, but this next stage is important. Anyone who gets in the way must be annihilated. Leave no trace of what happened. The detective and the boy are still major threats, and you must get rid of them while you can. This project cannot fail, it's what I've been waiting for my whole life. Just like you served him, you shall serve me. The YLO General has returned. Don't fail me.

- The Master

"Don't tell me that doesn't sound real!" Silvis exclaimed.

"Ugh," Junior whined.

"So Ghast is a YLO General," Silvis said.

"The YLO General," Junior said. "Sounds like he's much more important than it seems."

"What did the Master mean by 'him'?"

"I'm just as confused as you are," Junior said.

The two boys studied the letter for a while. It seemed very real, in Silvis' opinion. There were many things to wonder about, but one thing that confused Silvis the most and, at the same time, made him the most curious was the secret weapon. *What is this "secret weapon" thing? It's been forgotten for two centuries? Is that true or is it just figuratively speaking?*

"This weapon... I don't understand what they mean. But it does sound like it really is powerful. Whether they really have a weapon or not, we have to stop them," said Junior.

"And how are two boys gonna do that?" Silvis asked.

"There must be solutions. I'll be right back." Junior ran out of the room and Silvis heard things shuffling around. Thirty seconds later, Junior reappeared.

"I bought this from a kid about a week ago," he said, holding up the previous year's yearbook. "I was hoping it would help me identify and find my suspects. It'll definitely be handy now." He opened up the yearbook. The pages were fresh, like they were never opened before. He flipped pages until he found the start of the fourth grade classes.

The first page was Mrs. Coral's class from last year. Silvis and Junior knew some of these kids. A few of them, who were a group, used to pick on Silvis when he went to Newberry Park. Junior knew the same kids, since he was picked on, too. There were other kids they knew, but not Felix Westrough.

The next page was Mrs. Stacy's class. Silvis knew a few of these kids. After looking through everyone, Felix Westrough was at the end of the page. Silvis figured this was because his last name started with a "W." Felix Westrough was a redheaded, skinny, and pale boy. He had glasses that were too big for him and combed hair.

"Not what I was expecting..." Junior trailed off.

"This guy doesn't seem like a Wild Card at all—just someone who got A pluses in all the subjects," Silvis said.

"I'm afraid you're right. But we still don't know anything about him," Junior said.

"Then how are we supposed to find anything out about this guy?" Silvis wondered.

Junior thought for some time and then blurted, "I know!"

"What?" Silvis asked hastily.

"Didn't you say that Ghost told you he wants to help us?"

"Yeah, but how is he supposed to help us right now?"

"He's been in this school since T-K! He'll probably know who Westrough is."

"Oh!"

Junior sprinted away. A few seconds later, he came back with his computer. He opened it and clicked the calling icon on the bottom of the screen. There, in his contacts, was Ghost and his phone number. Junior clicked on Ghost and the computer began to dial.

Ten seconds later, Ghost picked up. Muffled noises were coming from his end. "Hey Junior, I don't have much time. I've got to ride to my friend's house in two minutes. I can call you back later," Ghost said quickly.

"Wait! It's something quick! I've just got a quick question," said Junior.

"Yeah? What is it?"

"You've been in this school for a while now, and I figured you'd know who a kid named Felix Westrough is? He was in last year's yearbook for fourth grade."

"Oh, Felix. He was my first friend in T-K. We used to always hang out and play together. People have made fun of him ever since second grade because of the way he looks. And they called him a nerd, since he always got good grades and bragged about them. One day in second grade, I told him a secret of mine, which I trusted him to know, but he betrayed me and told it to a group of kids I hated. Since then, we've been enemies. But the weirdest part about him is that he was expelled from school. No one knows why, but it was close to the end of the year last year."

"Whoa. That's a lot of information," Junior said.

"He was really expelled for no reason?" said Silvis.

"Yeah. I've got to go now. Maybe you can try and figure it out. Bye!"

"Hold—" Silvis sighed. "He's gone."

"This could be connected to the Griefings ..." Junior muttered.

"Junior?"

"Yeah?"

"I was thinking, what happened to Felix is similar to what happened to you."

"What do you mean?"

"Like when Mr. Williams fired you for no reason and hired Charlie. He was expelled for no reason, and maybe your experiences are connected.."

Junior stared at Silvis for a moment. *Does he think my idea is stupid? Does it make him think of something else?* Silvis wondered.

"Silvis," Junior said, "You're a genius! This could definitely be connected to what happened to me!"

Silvis grinned triumphantly. *He likes my idea. I guess I'm not such a bad detective after all.*

"Alright, Silvis, you should probably get going now. We can decide whether we're about to go into a prison of certain death tomorrow," said Junior.

Silvis nodded. "You're right."

"Have a good day!" Junior called as Silvis walked out the door.

•

The next morning at school, Silvis saw Ghost talking to Elly during recess at the snack benches.

"Oh, hey, Silvis!" Ghost called as Silvis approached him.

"Hey," he replied.

Elly spun around and stared at Silvis grimly. "What are you doing here?" she snapped. "Oh— you're Silvis... oh, right, the one who's helping us." Silvis was pretty sure he heard Elly mutter, "And the one who fell asleep during the meeting."

She forgot my name? She must not care about anyone.

"Yeah," Silvis replied. He put his focus towards Ghost as Elly walked away. "Hey, Ghost, I was wondering if you could tell me anything else you know about the Westrough kid."

"Oh, I was hoping Junior would try and figure it out."

"Well, we didn't have much time and we had very little information. Was Felix ever in trouble? Did he ever do bad things?" Silvis asked.

"Hmm, not really. Actually ..."

"What?"

"He always hated Mr. Williams, but that's all."

"Oh. Anything else about him?"

"Hmm ... no, not really."

"Alright, thanks for the information."

"No problem. Also, is there any time that you and Junior will be searching for clues or anything like that? I'd be more than glad to help."

Silvis stopped and thought for a moment. *Should I tell him? I think we can trust him, but Junior wouldn't like it if I told him.*

"No, not anytime soon. Well, see ya."

Ghost smiled at Silvis, and Silvis walked away.

•

Silvis's meeting at Junior's house was immediately after school. Once he arrived, he walked onto the front porch, which had a rocking chair on the right of the door and a mat that said, "Welcome."

Silvis rang the doorbell and heard nothing. He waited for a moment. Still nothing. Silvis rang the doorbell again.

After waiting a minute, nothing happened.

He decided to see if the door was unlocked and pulled the handle. The door opened and Silvis took off his shoes, then stepped inside.

"Hello?"

No response.

"Junior?"

Silvis sprinted around the house, searching.

"Junior!"

Nothing.

"Junior! This isn't funny!"

Still nothing.

"Where are you?!"

Silvis searched the kitchen, the living room, and Junior's room, but Junior wasn't anywhere. *What if Junior isn't here at all? What if he's in trouble? What if something bad happened? What if—*

Silvis stopped himself from finishing the what if. He knew it was bad, whatever it was. *Think positively,* he thought. Silvis cleared his mind and thought about all the places in Junior's house. *He has an attic. But no, he never goes up there, he can't even reach the ladder. So, if he isn't in the attic, then...*

"Basement!" Silvis shouted out loud. He sprinted over to the wall where the elevator door was located. The wall was quite big, but that wasn't Silvis's problem.

"How am I gonna find the button?! Where did I hit my head... where...." Silvis dragged his hand around the wall, looking for the small dent his head had made.

Suddenly, he remembered something. *The button wasn't around the elevator door, it was on it. I stumbled into the elevator after my head hit it.* He began tracing his hand on the area of the wall which the elevator was behind. After a few seconds, Silvis felt something very warm under a part of the wall. *This could be the button.* He left his hand in place and, a moment later, the wall sprung to the right and the elevator door opened. Silvis walked into the elevator.

Silvis looked around the elevator and saw the button that said "Basement," the only button in the elevator. He pressed the button and waited for it to go down.

Ding! As the elevator door slowly and annoyingly opened, Silvis peeked at the amazing laboratory basement. He saw several portraits, chemicals, tools, and bags. There were also a lot of unopened boxes, as if someone had moved into the house and left a lot of their belongings in the basement. But there was no Junior in sight.

He's gone, Silvis thought to himself. The doors fully opened, and he was about to enter the lab, when suddenly, he noticed something lying on the ground in the elevator. It was a piece of binder paper with something written on it. Silvis grabbed the binder paper and read it.

Silvis, the Wild Cards are here and I don't have time. They're gonna capture me so I left this note in the elevator and I hope you find it. If they're stupid enough, they might have left a letter somewhere in the house. If you can find my location, please try and rescue me. I'm this case's only hope. Sincerely, your detective friend, Junior.

Silvis stuffed the note in his pocket and jabbed his finger onto the button. Once the doors opened, he ran out of the elevator and around the house. He scanned the entire house again, looking for a note the Wild Cards may have left behind. Finally, he found a note lying on a chair at the dining table. It was also on binder paper, but it was folded. Silvis unfolded it and read it.

Hello, Silvis.

We have your detective friend. We are willing to negotiate and free your friend for something in return. We hope that you won't try and free him yourself, or things will be bad for you. He is being taken to Kiera's (the girl who betrayed you) house: 4478 Newbell Court. Come if you dare and we will make a deal.

From the Wild Cards, as you call us

Silvis could immediately tell that this was a trap. They weren't going to make a deal, they were just going to capture him. "But I have to rescue Junior," Silvis told himself. Whether it made him a fool or not, he was going to save Junior, and possibly Felix Westrough.

Silvis went back into the basement and searched the boxes. Silvis knew Junior never wanted him to look through his personal stuff, but this was an emergency. The first thing he found was an airsoft pistol, Silvis's airsoft pistol. He must've forgotten it at Newberry Park when they were chasing down the Wild Card. He grabbed it, only to see that there was only one magazine of five bullets inside.

Trying to wash away his bad thoughts and disappointment, Silvis quickly stuffed the pistol into his pocket and looked through the other boxes. He avoided the boxes with Junior's personal items and moved on to other ones, looking for anything he could use. Silvis kept searching but couldn't find anything.

After some time, Silvis found plain black gloves, which he wore, because they looked like spy gloves. Silvis also found an empty backpack. He thought it would have no use. *Think like a detective,* Silvis, he told himself. *If there is anything useful I find, I could put it in the backpack.* "Wow," Silvis muttered. "I really figured that out alone!"

Silvis ended up finding the confetti blaster and a flashlight. There was no need for a disguise, in Silvis's opinion, since the Wild Cards were already expecting him. Silvis put the blaster in his backpack and exited the basement.

Silvis rushed out Junior's front door and slammed it shut behind him. He ran to his bike and began to pedal. He knew where Newbell Court was, as it was only a minute's walk away from Newburg Street, where he lived.

Silvis biked toward his house desperately. He didn't know whether he would be able to pull this off, but trying was all he could do. The birds' chirping turned into owls' hooting as the sun began to set. Travelling in the darkness would be hard, but he had no choice.

After a couple of minutes, he reached Newburg Street. He looked around to see the houses and pine trees around him and navigated his way. He found the right path and biked toward it.

A minute later, he arrived at Newbell Court, which only had two working streetlights, one of them flickering. This made the street dark and, in his opinion, creepy. As the bright streetlight flickered and the wind howled loudly, Silvis continued on the street.

"Four-four-seven one, four-four-seven-two, four-four-seven-three, four-four-seven-four," he counted as he biked along the lane of houses slowly. Sure enough, he spotted four-four-seven-seven. "Here it is," he said to himself quietly, biking up to the next house. Then he realized he was out in the open, where everyone could see him. He took one foot off one of the pedals and steered the bike back a bit.

All the lights in the house were off, as if no one was there, which gave Silvis shivers. He took a closer look, then realized the house he was looking at was four-four-seven-nine. There was no four-four-seven-eight.

Silvis biked over to four-four-eight-zero. *But where's four-four-seven-eight?* He looked to his left, where he saw a large space of land with trees around it. It was a large field that took up the space of at least three houses, and in the middle was a large house made of very dark brown wood. It had large, square windows that were covered up by curtains. The house was dimly lit. It looked haunted, and Silvis was scared. He took a closer look at the house and saw the address:

four-four-seven-eight.

Silvis laid his bike against a tall tree, and its shadow made the bike very hard to see. It would be extremely hard to sneak into the house because the field around it was in plain sight. He crept behind the trees, getting closer and closer to the house, but he would still have to run through the field a bit, where he could definitely be spotted.

Silvis kneeled behind a tree and prepared to sprint over to the house, when suddenly—creeeeak! He nearly fell over in fear. "This house is definitely haunted!" he whispered loudly.

Silvis peered over at the house, where he saw two kids in morph suit masks, definitely Wild Cards, walk out of the front door. They wore normal clothes, but they both had a walkie talkie sticking out of their pants' pockets. Silvis figured he must've whispered too loudly, because they suddenly looked his way. He immediately jutted his head back behind the tree. There's no way I'm gonna be able to do this. I'm definitely screwed.

Fortunately for Silvis, the kids wearing the morph suit masks ignored the noise, probably because they thought it was just the howling wind.
Silvis heard footsteps. He stuck his head out a bit to see the Wild Cards running towards the street. A moment later, they were out of his eyesight, but Silvis heard a scraping noise.

The Wild Cards were back, each pulling a garbage bin behind them. They went towards the house. When they were halfway there, one of them picked up their walkie talkie. They listened for a second, then said something to the other Wild Card. They immediately scrambled towards the house and went inside.

This is my chance. Silvis ran towards one of the garbage bins, being as quiet as he could while also being quick. He lifted the lid and tried climbing in. With some struggle, Silvis eventually got in and pulled the lid shut.

Although there was no trash in the garbage bin, it still stunk a ton. Silvis wanted to hurtle out the trash bin and charge towards the house, beating up all the Wild Cards, but he knew that wasn't wise.

What felt like an eternity (but was actually a minute) later, footsteps came towards the trash bin and Silvis let out a sigh of relief. His bin was now being pulled, and he could hear the other bin being pulled, too.

"I hate this job," Silvis heard one of the Wild Cards say.

"Well, it wasn't our choice," Silvis heard the other Wild Card say, who had a much deeper voice. "We were forced to do this."

They were forced into the job. I wonder how many others were too.

After a few seconds, the garbage bin stopped moving. "Finally, the backyard," Silvis heard the Wild Card with the deeper voice say.

"Now we gotta go to that Ghast guy for more orders."

The Wild Cards ran away, and Silvis's heart skipped a beat. He felt like he was an ocean, and all his courage was washed ashore. *Ghast is here. The YLO general. The one who attacked Junior and wants both of us dead. I can't do this. He's gonna do something horrible if he finds me.*

Silvis forced himself not to think about Ghast and continue. He sat in the stinky garbage bin for two minutes, until he was sure no one was around. He slowly used his head to push open the lid of the bin, just enough to scout for any Wild Cards. No one was there.

Silvis crept out of the bin and looked around. A lamp hung from the roof, lighting up the whole backyard. He noticed the backyard door, a glass sliding door that was halfway open, enough for him to fit through.

He slowly tiptoed towards the backyard door and looked inside the house. In front of him was a living room with a small old-looking TV and couches to sit on. To the left of the living room, he could see stairs, and a few feet away from the living room was the front door, where a Wild Card wearing a morph suit mask stood with their back turned.

It's now or never. Silvis rushed towards the stairs quietly, and the Wild Card didn't hear him. His excitement was quickly washed away when he heard creaking from upstairs. *There must be a bunch of Wild Cards up there. Think Silvis, think.*

As Silvis crouched at the first step of the stairs, he realized what to do. It was the same way he escaped the last time: a distraction. He whipped his backpack off of his back and slowly unzipped it.

"Did the bees get in the house again?" Silvis heard the Wild Card at the door bark in an annoyed tone.

Uh oh. Silvis stuck his hand in the backpack after unzipping it halfway and pulled out the first thing he touched, the airsoft pistol. *What could I use this for... I could shoot someone. That would distract everyone.*

The Wild Card standing at the door must have heard him. The Wild Card walked into Silvis's view, but he didn't see Silvis yet. Silvis aimed, and footsteps rushed in his direction from upstairs. His stomach lurched, and he suddenly pulled the trigger and dropped the pistol. The pellet from the gun whizzed right past the Wild Card's head and the pistol hit the ground with a loud bang. Silvis didn't need to look to see what had happened.

"There's a gun!" the Wild Card screamed. "Someone has a gun! Everyone, run for your life!"

Uh oh. Silvis ran up the stairs and rushed into the first room he saw, which was on his right. There was a bunk bed in the room, but otherwise it was empty. He ran to the bed and slid under it. Loud footsteps thundered down the stairs as people shouted at each other.

"Where's the gun?!" someone yelled.

"Shouldn't we be running from it?" another said.

"Who has the gun?!" the yells continued.

If only they knew it was just an airsoft pistol. But that wouldn't help me at all.

All of a sudden, Silvis heard footsteps coming from the room he was in. He heard whispering and then footsteps coming closer to bed. Two pairs of big feet were standing in front of the bed. *I need to get out of here,* Silvis realized. He began to wriggle to the other side of the bed, but it was too late. Strong hands seized Silvis's arm and pulled him out from under the bed.

"Aha!" a voice taunted, throwing Silvis onto the floor.

Standing above him was a man who looked extremely scary, wearing a black vest with "YLO" on it and his mask with X's on it. Ghast. He was the one person Silvis wanted to avoid! Silvis trembled in fear on the inside, but forced himself to look strong, like he knew what he was doing and he wasn't afraid.

"Get up, boy!" Ghast snapped as he pulled Silvis up from the ground. "You think you're so slick, huh? Putting those two annoying twins in jail and spying on us in the school?"

"I'm not afraid of you or any of your stupid Wild Cards!" Silvis forced himself to shout back.

"Ah, you say that, boy. Don't you worry, this'll be the last day you see 'em or anyone else!"

Silvis' mind raced for a creative solution. *A distraction. I'll need a distraction to escape.* Acting fast, Silvis pointed to the door and screamed as loud as could, "GAH!"

"What?" Ghost bellowed in confusion and annoyance, turning to face the door.

After seeing nothing at the door, Ghost turned back to look at him. Silvis threw a punch at Ghost's face so hard that he felt like he had just punched a rock. With his numb hand, he quickly threw his backpack on the ground, unzipped it, and grabbed the confetti blaster from it. Ghost was clutching his mask at the spot where his nose was, blood raining from his mask while he roared in pain and rage.

"I'll kill you, boy, I'll kill you!" Ghost threatened.

"Not today!" Silvis taunted and loaded the confetti blaster. Silvis aimed the blaster at Ghost's face, and before Ghost could say anything, he pulled the trigger. A wave of confetti, all the colors of the rainbow and each very small, blasted into Ghost's mask in less than a second.

"Ahhh!" Ghost yelled. Silvis seized the opportunity and ran out of the room, through the hall of rooms up the stairs to the third floor. *Felix said the prison was in an attic...*

"He's escaping! The one who has the gun! Get him!" Ghost called as Silvis ran away.

Silvis rushed through the hall and looked at all the doors. There were different labels on them, such as the break room, storage room, and planning room.

Footsteps thumped up the stairs and five different Wild Cards arrived all at once. Silvis shot the confetti launcher straight at them. The confetti went straight at their faces, covered in morph suit masks, and they waved their hands to get it away.

In the brief moment that the Wild Cards were distracted, Silvis found the door that was labeled "Prison." He opened the big wooden door. Wild Cards were inches behind him and he could feel hands reaching for him.

Silvis shut the door quickly as the five Wild Cards tried to get inside. He locked the doorknob before looking at his surroundings. The prison was an unlit, dusty room with many storage boxes and prison cells that were built into the attic walls. Inside the prison cells were many large adults and teenagers who looked like real prisoners. He looked around to find his detective friend as the Wild Cards banged on the door, trying to get in.

"Silvis?" That voice was definitely Junior's. "You came!"

"Junior! I found you!" Silvis couldn't see Junior very well in the dark room and he couldn't find the light switch, but he could still see a spark of hope light up on Junior's face.

"There's no time, Silvis! We gotta get out of here!"

"What about all these others?"

"There's no time! And believe me, most of these people deserve to be here. Just bring Felix and me and let's go!"

"No, boy! Break us out now!" a prisoner roared.

"No, break me out!" another yelled.

Junior said, "Silvis, the Wild Cards will come in any time now, we gotta go!"

Feeling very guilty, Silvis rushed over to Junior's cell. Junior was wearing the same clothes as earlier that day, but his whole body was very dusty and he looked like he was going to pass out if he didn't get food.

Inside the cell next to Junior's was a tall, skinny, and scrawny boy with combed hair and oversized glasses, just like the picture in the yearbook. He was wearing a plain white shirt that was so dusty that it looked kind of gray.

"Someone's finally came! Woo hoo, it's been sooo long!" Felix Westrough cheered. "How'd you do it?! I've been calculating all the possibilities of how we could escape, but the chances were super low that someone would break into this house and help us escape—let alone someone by themself!"

This kid wasn't too annoying, in Silvis's opinion. *How is anyone supposed to answer all his questions?* Silvis unlocked Felix's and Junior's cells.

"What're you doing, boy? Break us out, too!" another prisoner cried.

"Yeah, break me out! It's been so long!" called another.

Silvis heard Junior opening the only window in the dusty room and took a guilty look at the prisoners.

"We're supposed to go through the window?" Silvis complained as he stared down at the part of the roof under the room. It would be a very long fall, and he'd possibly break a lot of bones.

"Stop complaining!" Junior scolded. "It'll be fine."

"Alright, then," Silvis replied, swallowing his fear.

"Pretty high fall. There's a decent chance we could get hurt if we fall," Felix said.

"Then we just won't fall!" said Junior, who took the first step, and although he was quite fearless when he did it, Silvis could see some fear and hesitation in him. He took the next step and had his full body on the roof.

"How are we gonna get down?" Silvis asked.

"Once you get to the edge, you gotta hang onto the platform and then drop down so it's a small fall," Felix explained.

"Yikes," Silvis said out loud.

Junior walked to the ledge and then hung down. A moment later, he let go and almost landed on his feet. "It doesn't hurt!" Junior confirmed. Felix went next and he did all of it in ten seconds (Silvis was counting), which impressed Silvis. Next, it was Silvis's turn. He took a few deep breaths, getting himself prepared. He ran to the edge and looked down. Felix and Junior were there staring at him hopefully. You can do this, Silvis. He hung onto the edge and dropped down a second later. The fall didn't hurt much at all.

"We gotta go now!" Junior told them.

"What about you and Felix? I only brought my own bike!"

"We can go on foot!" Felix suggested. "If we're fast enough, they won't know which way we went. There's no way they could follow us."

"Alright, then. You guys go on foot, I'll bike home," Silvis agreed.

"That works," Junior said.

"I'm so excited to see my family again!" said Felix. "Thanks for breaking me out, uh..."

"Silvis," said Silvis.

"Silvis," Felix repeated. He then sprinted away.

"Thanks for saving me, Silvis," said Junior, shuffling on his feet.

"No problem," said Silvis. "Now let's get going so they don't catch us!"

CHAPTER 10
YLO GENERAL

The next morning, Silvis made it to school just before the bell rang. He slipped into class quickly, as his class line had already left for the classroom. Silvis was sure Junior was just as tired as he was after last night's escape, and Junior wasn't here yet. Five minutes later, after the class was already sitting in a circle on the rainbow rug and doing their morning meeting, Junior finally showed up. He sat down next to Silvis and whispered, "I have an update on the case. Meet me at my place right after school."

The day went by, and finally, it was time. He biked to Junior's house right when the bell rang and waited for Junior for two minutes until Junior arrived.

"I have some new security measures for my house," said Junior as they approached the front door and punched in a code on a keypad that Silvis had never seen before. "There is a special setting on the door that activates a trap (a bucket of slime and an alarm) if anyone is acting suspicious." Junior shut the door behind him as he and Silvis walked into the house and pulled the bolt so that the door was completely break-in-proof.

"Cool," said Silvis. "So, what's new with the case?"

Junior walked over to a cabinet in the living room that was next to the fireplace and typed in the code (it also had a lock). Once it was open, Junior pulled out an envelope.

"This was on my doorstep when I got home last night," he said, showing Silvis the envelope. "I waited to open it until you were here." He tore it open and they read it together.

Dear Junior, Silvis, Elly, and Willow,

Hello. My name is Mr. Stevenson. I know that all the kids fear me and call me the Hawkman, but I am nothing to fear. I believe I can help you, as I know a lot of information that might be useful for your case. Please come to my house, 678 Newburg Street at 6:00 P.M. on Wednesday, October 15th. I'm not the bad guy in this, and I know about someone that I know you miss. Please come.

Sincerely, Mr. Stevenson/The Hawkman

One week later, it was October the fifteenth, the day that Silvis and Junior were going to the Hawkman's house and a week after they got the letter. They'd been laying low since breaking Junior and Felix out of prison, only leaving the house to go to school. Felix had come back to school, and police were investigating why he had gone missing. Apparently, the Wild Cards had abandoned Kiera's foster parents' house, so there wasn't any evidence for what Felix said, and the police couldn't find anyone who was involved in his disappearance. Thankfully, there hadn't been any more Griefings in Hillstretch. The week had been surprisingly normal.

Junior and Silvis were waiting at Junior's house for the others to arrive. "They should be here any—" Junior began.

Ding! Dingdingdingdingding!

"Coming, coming!" Junior called as he rushed to the door. He pulled a curtain on a window that was next to the door and then walked over to the door, pulled the bolt, and opened the lock.

Elly and Willow stood outside the door. "Hey guys!" Willow greeted cheerfully.

Elly, who had her hands crossed and wore a large frown, snorted. Although she was annoying, Elly was still the one who hired Junior, after all, and the Hawkman wanted her to come, too. "The last thing I wanna do is go to some crazy guy's house, but it's for Zak, so whatever," she said.

"Hey, why isn't Ghost here?" asked Willow.

"The Hawkman didn't address the letter to him," said Junior. "So I didn't tell him about it."

"That's weird," said Willow. "He should know that we're all friends working on the case together. I've mentioned it to him before."

Junior shrugged and then explained to the girls what they were going to do and how he was armed, pulling out the confetti blaster.

"With that thing?" Elly complained, looking at the blaster. "What's that gonna do?"

"A lot more than you think," Junior replied. The four of them set off together on foot toward the Hawkman's house.

The fall breeze had started, and it was getting cold in Hillstretch City. At the moment, the breeze wasn't too cold and felt very nice as it blew in Silvis's hair. *I wonder what the Hawkman's got to say. Is this a trick? The confetti blaster won't do much, I'm not sure how we'll escape this if it is a trap,* Silvis thought. *I'm not sure if I could trust the Hawkman, although he seems like a genuine guy. Or what if the rumors are true and he's really crazy?*

"Silvis," Junior whispered while they were walking so the girls couldn't hear.

"What?" Silvis replied.

"I need to tell you something."

"Tell me, then."

"The confetti blaster... it's not what you think. There's another mode on it. If you switch it on, the confetti is sticky, and it will stick to whoever you shoot and sting their skin."

"Are you serious?" Silvis asked in shock. "Why didn't you tell me? It would've helped me so much when I rescued—"

"Shh! Someone's gonna hear you!"

When they arrived at the Hawkman's house, Junior rang the doorbell. The door was opened a moment later by a tall, middle-aged man who was wearing a large sheepskin coat and a plain white shirt under it. The man had lime green eyes and had a bushy, thick beard.

"Hello!" the man said cheerfully. Although he looked very creepy to Silvis, he seemed nice and welcoming. "Hello, Willow, it's great to meet your friends in person! I'm Mr. Stevenson, but you can call me Hawkman if you want."

"Hi, there, sir, it's great to meet you," Junior greeted politely and then shook the Hawkman's hand.

"Come in, I'll lead you to my meeting room."

Everyone said hi to the Hawkman and he led them around his house. The Hawkman's house was cozy, with couches and a fireplace that was lit on the right of the door. He had a Christmas tree set up. The floors were marble, and there were many rooms on the first floor.

How much about this guy does Willow know? Does she know for sure that he's actually safe and this isn't a trap? Silvis thought.

"What do you do for him?" Silvis whispered to Willow when the Hawkman went to check on something. Everyone knew that Willow worked for the Hawkman, but not much about her work was specified.

"I'm kinda like a maid," Willow said, embarrassed. "I clean most of his house for him, and I help him with some simple chores. He's actually a pretty nice guy."

Junior, who had listened to what she said, remarked, "Interesting."

The Hawkman led the kids to a hall on the first floor that had three different doors. He pointed to the door in the middle and told them, "This is my meeting and office room where we'll talk."

The kids nodded.

"Please don't go in that room, it's my personal room." The Hawkman pointed to the door to the left of the middle room.

"So," the Hawkman began after everyone was seated. "Let's get right into it."

"Ahem," Junior said, catching everyone's attention. "Oh, I was just clearing my throat."

"Anyways," the Hawkman continued, slightly annoyed. "I heard that you kids are investigating the Griefings and you have a kid detective."

"Me," Junior confirmed.

"Yes, I know."

"So, why'd you bring us here?" Silvis asked impolitely, desperate to get to the point.

"Because I know a thing or two about what you're investigating—and what you're getting into," the Hawkman added.

"Ah," Junior said. "You don't want us to continue this, do you? Well, sorry, sir, we're going to continue this case, respectfully."

The Hawkman smiled faintly. "It's much more than that. I've found out a few things. Things that you'd definitely want to know, about a deadly weapon and a long-lost boy."

"Zak," Elly muttered under her breath. "You found Zak?"

The Hawkman shook his head. "No. I don't know who Zak is, but I heard of someone else." He looked at Junior, who shifted uncomfortably.

"Oh," Elly replied, disappointedly.

"Are you serious? Really?" Junior blurted in shock. He looked like he wanted to get up, storm over to the Hawkman, and bomb him with questions.

"The boy I am talking about is a teenager who went missing two years ago. I've seen him a few times at the paintball field, and I think I know who it is," the Hawkman explained.

Missing for two years? As weird as it was, it was awfully familiar.

"Bear," Junior whispered to himself in disbelief. "It's Bear."

Bear? Junior's lost brother? That's impossible!

"A while ago, he left a letter in the forest next to the paintball field that had your name on it. Clearly, he was hoping you'd find it and read it, but the crazy people you call Wild Cards burned it and I have no idea why."

"Bear is alive. We have to go find him!" said Junior. He stood up.

"Whoa, whoa, whoa. Slow it down there," Elly interrupted. "You have a brother that's been missing for two years and you said nothing about it? And now we're all supposed to go find this missing guy?"

"I don't care whether you wanna help or not! I'm finding him!" Junior spat at Elly. She glared back at him.

"Calm down, kids. Junior, you can't go there. It's far too dangerous there, I saw many Wild Cards in that area," the Hawkman said.

"It's much worse, there's also Ghast there!" Silvis added, still confused about Bear.

"Ghast?" the Hawkman said quickly.

"Yeah, what's Ghast?" Elly asked.

Uh oh.

"It's—it's not important," said Silvis.

"I want to know! Willow and Junior, why aren't you saying anything? Are you guys keeping secrets from me?" said Elly.

"I have that letter from Bear for you, Junior. It's upstairs, I'll go get it now. Stay here."

"A letter from Bear! Yes! Please go get it!"

"I will." The Hawkman left the room, leaving the door open, and walked upstairs.

"Quick, let's go to his private room!" Elly whispered once he was out of view.

"Elly! Respect his privacy!" Willow whispered back.

"I don't care, I'm going anyway!"

"I'm going, too. I don't entirely trust that guy," Junior said.

"What! Guys, he said—" said Willow. But Elly and Junior were already walking out of the room.

I guess I'll go, too. Silvis followed behind them. He was also suspicious of the Hawkman, and although he knew it was wrong to snoop, he was also very curious.

"We gotta be real quiet," Junior whispered as Elly slowly opened the door without making any noise.

Inside was a messy room with papers sprawled all over a large table and desk. A glass box lay on top of the table, next to stuffed shelves. Silvis shivered when he saw what was inside the glass box.

It was Ghast's mask, with X's for eyes and a creepy smile.

"That's—I—" Silvis said, his heart pumping fast.

"Elly, get back in the other room, we need to get out of here right now," said Junior.

Silvis never recalled a time that he saw Junior this serious. Gratefully, Elly must've noticed Junior's seriousness, too, because she left without protesting.

The trio walked back into the room and sat down without a word. A moment later, the Hawkman's footsteps came down the stairs and he appeared in the room. "Sorry, Junior, I couldn't find the note. But I—"

"It was great to meet with you and thanks a lot for the information but we have a meeting with the principal about something we all did at class and, y'know, we can't miss a meeting with the principal and we're already five minutes late so we've really got to go," Junior lied.

"Oh, okay. Perhaps we could meet later?"

"Yeah, definitely, we'll come back sometime soon," said Junior.

"Alright, guys. Bye."

After they left, they immediately all rushed to a field that was far away and out of view from the Hawkman's house, where they knew it was safe to talk.

"Can you guys tell me what the heck is going on?" Elly yelled. "I'm tired of all these secrets and weird stuff!"

"Willow, did you ever go into the Hawkman's personal room?" Junior demanded.

"No," said Willow. "W-what did you find in there?"

"To make it simple for you, the Hawkman is Ghast, a creepy Wild Card general who wears a mask with X's for eyes and a creepy smile," said Junior.

"Mr. Stevenson is a Wild Card?" Willow whispered.

"Yes," said Junior. "And he knows where Bear is."

"Your long-lost brother?" said Elly.

Junior nodded.

"What if the YLO have something to do with his disappearance?" said Silvis.

"I think you're exactly right, Silvis," said Junior. "We have to look for him."

"Tonight?" shrieked Elly. "It's dark already!"

"We don't have a choice," said Junior. "The Hawkman might already suspect we know he's Ghast. He's no fool."

"Well, I have to go to ballet practice, so I'll pass on this one," said Elly, taking out her phone.

"Silvis? Willow?" said Junior.

"I'll come," said Silvis.

"Me, too," said Willow.

Elly's mom picked her up and drove her home. The other three set off for the paintball field.

"You guys?" said Junior, his voice quiet.

"What?" Willow and Silvis said.

"I think it's time I tell you my real name. It's Zach, just like Zak, but spelled 'Z-A-C-H' instead of 'Z-A-K.'"

"Woah," said Silvis. "Why are you telling us now?"

"Don't you think it's weird that my brother went missing, and then a kid named Zak went missing? Elly didn't know Bear and I don't know Zak, but what if ... what if they're the same person?"

Silvis gasped. "I guess we'll have to find out."

CHAPTER 11

BEAR

They approached the woods next to the paintball field. No one had been in it for a while and people said it was haunted. Silvis spied a hut in the center of the field.

"That's Ghast's hut. We gotta find a way to destroy him," Junior said, pointing to the hut.

"How are we supposed to destroy him?" Silvis asked.

"With a plan, of course, and with the confetti blaster," said Junior.

"It's really strong enough to destroy someone?" said Willow.

"You underestimate it. Wait 'till you see it in action."

The kids entered the woods next to the paintball field. Junior unzipped his backpack and took out the confetti blaster.

"Bear is supposed to be somewhere here? In literally the middle of nowhere?" Silvis said doubtfully. "What have I gotten into? I used to never talk to anyone, and now I'm searching for someone who's been missing for two years with a kid detective."

"Well, you sure are helping a lot of people, whether you like it or not," Junior pointed out.

"Junior's right," said Willow.

There was a scattering sound nearby, and Junior lifted up the blaster in caution. He flipped a switch on the side of it, which Silvis guessed was to change it to sticky mode.

"Keep a lookout," Junior whispered to Silvis.

Silvis nodded and looked around.

Suddenly, a figure sprung out from behind a bush and charged towards them with a steel bat.

"AH!" Willow screamed.

Junior loaded the confetti blaster and pulled the trigger. A rainbow-colored pellet that looked much like a paintball zipped through the air and hit the figure right in the chest. The pellet immediately broke into pieces, launching confetti onto the figure's body and sticking onto their black hoodie.

"Wow," Silvis muttered silently. "That's awesome."

The person was wearing a morph suit mask. They were definitely a Wild Card and definitely a kid. "AHHH! GAH! Help! It stings!" the Wild Card screamed in agony.

"That must be so painful," Silvis said, feeling bad for the Wild Card. Junior watched the Wild Card as he screeched in pain and then fell to the ground. His body went limp.

"There," Junior said.

"Did he pass out? Is he okay?" said Willow.

"He's definitely not okay, and I don't know whether he passed out or not." Junior loaded the deadly confetti blaster and walked over to the Wild Card cautiously. He bent down and pulled off the Wild Cards mask. The Wild Card had the face of a boy named Devin, a very big know-it-all and snitch in their grade. His eyes were glued shut; he had clearly passed out from the pain.

"Devin's a Wild Card!" Silvis said in disbelief.

"Devin would never choose to be a Wild Card, they must've forced him," Willow said.

"Don't assume. You never know who might be a traitor," said Junior. "Maybe he's changed."

"I guess you're right," said Willow. "I never would've guessed Mr. Stevenson..."

Silvis patted her shoulder. She was obviously still shocked at the Hawkman's betrayal.

132

Junior looked around. "Hmm. I wish we could turn him in or something, but there's no evidence. I'll leave a note on him from me," said Junior.

Since Junior had a sticky note pad in his backpack, he jotted down a letter on a sticky note that said:

> *Your weak Wild Card failed to stop me. He could've done it, beat me and won, but no, he failed, just like you guys and your plans.*

Junior stuck the note onto Devin's hoodie and then he, Silvis, and Willow dragged Devin to Ghast's hut, where they could only pray that Devin wouldn't wake up before Ghast arrived. They then went back to where they had been in the forest and continued on a path.

After walking for some time, they stopped. "It's a fork," Junior noted.

Junior held up the confetti blaster. "Alright, you two go to the right and I'll go to the left. If anything happens, scream for me."

"All I can say is good luck, I guess," said Silvis.

"Yeah, yell if you need our help," said Willow.

"Same to you," said Junior.

Silvis and Willow continued along the path. Soon, Junior was out of range and they couldn't hear him anymore. *What if something happens? Will Junior ever even find me? Or what if something happens to Junior? How am I gonna know?* Silvis tried to relax himself, but the tension wouldn't leave his mind.

There were shrubs, bushes, and trees all around them. This was very similar to the forest he and Junior had hid in when the Wild Cards had chased them at Newberry Park. The path seemed like it was endless. They walked in silence to be as quiet as possible.

Silvis and Willow walked for five more minutes until they reached a dead end, where the paths finally connected. *I hope Junior is there. I hope he wasn't captured by Wild Cards.* There was a path in between two bushes that Junior must've gone through.

"Alright, he must be here," he said. They walked through the path to see another path, where they saw someone ahead.

"Hey! Junior! Is that you?"

The person turned around, and sure enough, it was Junior.

Phew. he's okay. Everything's gonna be fine.

"I'm happy you're both alright," Junior said. "Did you run into any Wild Cards?"

"Nope," said Willow.

"Me neither," said Junior.

The kids walked through the path until Junior noticed a bush that seemed out of place. "I think there's something behind it," Junior observed. "I'll go check." He walked through the large, light green bush until he got to the other end. "It's not exactly a path, but it's a clearing. I think we're on the right track!" The kids walked through the bush to see a clearing with vines hanging from the trees and bushes all around. "Continue along the clearing, but watch out," Junior said.

The kids continued along the clearing until Willow noticed another odd bush. "That doesn't look right," Willow observed. Without saying anything, she rushed through the bushes and ran to the other side.

"Willow! Wait!" said Silvis. "You don't know what's—" He zipped through the bush after her. When he got to the other side, he saw her standing in front of him. "Willow! What are you doing?"

"I just wanted to make sure it was safe before you came through," she said.

"Oh. Junior, it's safe!"

Junior rushed through the bushes to meet them. They were standing in another clearing, but this time, it looked even more foresty.

"Whoa," Junior said. "We must be on the right track"

After continuing on the new clearing for some time, it seemed like it was coming to an end. "Watch out!" Junior yelled as Silvis began to take another step.

"What?" Silvis asked.

"It's a trap." Junior reached his hand down to the vine on the floor and stuck his hand through it. Under it was a large ditch that Silvis would've been trapped in if it wasn't for Junior.

"Wow. That was close."

The kids walked around the ditch and kept walking for a few more minutes. Thick vines were at the end, signaling that this was the end of the clearing.

"There could be more behind this," Junior whispered. He quietly pushed the vines aside, and Silvis and Willow followed. Silvis didn't know whether the Wild Cards had made this trap or someone else had, but if it was the Wild Cards, it would be trouble. Junior raised the confetti blaster, ready to shoot if something happened.

They were in front of a large grass field with a shed, a small cabin, and a bike, with tons of vines all around. "Wow," Junior muttered.

"I'll go," Silvis volunteered. He took a step forward. Vines from the right and left shot at his feet and wrapped around them. "AH!" he screamed.

A tall figure charged towards him, fists clenched.

Silvis closed his eyes and braced for pain. *Is this how it ends? Is this how I die?*

Junior yelled, "Wait!"

The person looked at Junior and Willow and unclenched his fists. "Junior?" he said in disbelief.

"Bear? We found you! Oh my... How are you?" Through the leaves and vines around his face, Silvis could see tears streaming down Junior's face.

"You came here to find me?" Bear asked. "After two years... You found me, brother," Bear spread his arms and Junior hugged him. Bear was a tall and muscular guy wearing a gray tank top full of sweat and black sweatpants.

"I thought I'd never see you again," said Junior.

Silvis was still lying on the ground trapped by Bear's vines. *Hello! I'm right here! Can't you just free me?* He didn't want to ruin the moment, so he didn't say anything.

Lucky for Silvis, Junior introduced him and Willow to Bear and Bear took out a pocketknife to cut the vines.

"Sorry about that," Bear said. "The only visitors I get around here are the YLO."

"What?" Junior asked. "The YLO are—"

"I've got a lot to tell you."

"No, I've probably got even more." Junior grinned at Bear and Bear grinned back.

"Let's go inside," said Bear.

Bear's cabin was warm and cozy, but very small. It had only one bedroom. There were coats and animal skins on the wooden walls and a large fire burned in the fireplace. He had a small kitchen and a TV above the fireplace. There were two cozy couches in front of the TV. The kids sat down.

"Junior never really made friends," Bear told Silvis and Willow. "But look where you've gotten without me!"

"We don't have all the time in the world, Bear," Junior reminded him.

"Right. Looks like it's explaining time."

"The YLO are an evil crime group that has lasted for hundreds of years. Our father was a famous investigator; he's the one who trained Junior. For years, our father investigated the crimes of the YLO and tried to uncover who they were and who their leader was. He caught so many of their members, and he was always on their trail. But the YLO don't like to be messed with. So they killed him."

"What?!" Junior bellowed. "The Wild Cards killed our father?"

Bear nodded his head sadly. "I didn't want to tell you because you were so young. I'm sorry I lied to you. But Dad left me a mission, to take them down. So that's what I went to do, two years ago. The YLO tried to kill me, and I barely escaped. Since then, I had no choice but to hide."

"Why didn't you come home?" said Junior. "I've thought you were dead all this time."

"I didn't want you to be in danger. That's not what Dad would have wanted. I'm sorry."

"They killed him..." said Junior.

Bear put an arm around Junior's back. "It's okay, Junior, we can't reverse it, but we can avenge him."

"We do know some stuff about the Wild—I mean, the YLO," said Junior. Junior explained to Bear everything they had been through, from the Griefings to their confrontation with the Hawkman/Ghast.

"I knew you'd make use of that letter I sent you!" Bear cheered triumphantly.

"What letter?" Junior asked.

"The one with the clues."

"What?! You knew all that stuff, but you didn't actually tell me?"

"I wanted to make a real mystery, Junior. Of course, you figured out most of it, since you're a great detective."

"I guess that's a valid reason."

Valid reason? We could've known so much if he had given Junior real information!

"But the note said that Elly is related to Zak, but she doesn't know about it. What's that supposed to mean?" Silvis asked.

Bear sighed. "I am Zak. I figured you'd know Elly, since she told me everyone at school knows her," Bear said. "And Elly is our cousin. It's something I found out while I was out here trying to take down the Wild Cards."

"Wait, what? That bossy grump is our cousin?" said Junior.

"Don't talk about my friend like that!" Willow defended.

"Sorry," said Junior. "I'm just shocked!"

"There's only one last thing," Bear said.

"What is it?" Junior asked.

"The YLO, or Wild Cards, as you call them, they have a secret superweapon."

"Is it the one mentioned in the letter to Ghast?"

"I believe so. All I know is that it's a deadly instrument, I believe a violin. It can be charged and shoots out a very powerful beam."

Silvis tried not to gasp. *I have a violin that shoots out a powerful beam!* Then he had a worse thought: *Were my parents part of the YLO? Do I have the YLO's secret superweapon?*

Bear continued, "I have no idea how old it is, but this thing can probably destroy almost anything. And if we're gonna stop the YLO, we have to find this weapon and destroy it."

"Or we could use it to destroy them," Junior suggested. "A violin that shoots beams of something! That's crazy!"

I have to say something. It's the right thing to do.

"Guys," Silvis said.

"I'm not a guy!" Willow scoffed.

"Sorry. This is important, though. Very important. You have to come with me."

CHAPTER 12

UNVEILED

Silvis's thoughts exploded. *This can't be happening. What's going on? Why is this happening to me? This violin's not even mine! Ugh, I don't understand any of this!*

"Why are we in your bedroom?" Bear asked.

"Yeah, can you tell us why we're here already?" Junior added.

"Okay, okay," Silvis answered nervously. He looked down at the bottom drawer, which had a lock on it, and punched the code into the lock. The lock opened and Silvis pulled the drawer open. He took out the Sapphire Mando's case and placed it on his bed.

"Whoa," Bear said.

"That's cool... but what's so important about this?" Junior said impatiently.

"You'll see," Silvis reassured. He opened up the case and inside was the beautiful gray and blue Sapphire Mando.

"Wow!" Willow said.

"Are those made of sapphire?" Bear asked, pointing to the strings on the Sapphire Mando.

"Have any of you heard of the Sapphire Mando?" Silvis asked.

"Sapphire Mando—sounds familiar ... wait, isn't it the best violin in the world or something?" Junior asked.

Silvis nodded.

"Wait—is that it?!" Willow exclaimed.

"It sure is," Silvis replied.

"Isn't it worth, like, thirty million dollars?" Junior asked in surprise.

"It's priceless to me," Silvis said. He pointed to behind the bridge of the violin, where his name was etched onto the wood.

"Oh my God, how does it have your name on it?" Willow gasped.

"I don't know. I found this in my basement a few weeks ago. My whole family was really good at the violin, and they taught me how to play it. My mother's name was carved into the violin before mine. Tt was covered by the diamond dust when I found it."

"Wait," Bear said. "Is that the secret weapon?"

●

In the backyard, it was dark, but the Sapphire Mando glimmered in the night sky. As the others watched him, Silvis played a song on the violin. He aimed the scroll at a tree, played a melody for a few seconds, and then played a long E note. A zapping noise echoed through the air. A beam of dark blue shot out from the sapphire on the scroll right into the tree, creating a small hole that went all the way through the tree trunk.

"Holy crap!" Bear yelled. "That thing is insane!"

"It looks like it's shooting electricity," said Junior.

"Yeah," said Bear. "Try playing a bit longer this time."

Silvis did what Bear told him. The blue beam was thicker and louder.

"Hmm," said Bear. "It seems like playing a long note is what shoots the electricity. And the longer you play before that, the stronger the beam will be."

"Cool," said Willow. "How'd this end up in your basement?"

"I have no idea, but it seems just like the superweapon," Silvis said.

"But how? It's not the Wild Cards', it's yours!" Willow said.

"I guess my parents must have been Wild Cards," said Silvis, ashamed. "Maybe Junior's dad took them to jail."

"Or," Junior suggested, "the Wild Cards have another violin just like yours with the same powers ... but that's just a theory."

"I like that theory," said Silvis, relieved.

"It's really late," said Bear. "We should all get some sleep."

Willow, Junior, and Bear went home. Silvis played the Sapphire Mando some more and then finally went to bed.

●

The next day after school, Junior gathered Willow, Bear, and Silvis in his living room and began his speech. "Alright, guys. If we're gonna pull this off, three eleven-year-olds and one seventeen-year-old versus an entire army of Wild Cards, we're gonna have to do this neatly. Our first target is Ghast, but we have to make sure nobody finds out about the violin, or we're dead. The plan is simple: we'll go to the paintball field. We'll each have confetti blasters and Silvis will have the Sapphire Mando. We'll all sneak up on the target; me, Willow, and Bear will make a distraction so we can find Ghast, and then we'll all blast him at once with our weapons," Junior explained.

"Sounds like a good plan," Silvis said.

There wasn't a moment to waste. They all wore camo clothes so that it would be easier to blend in with their surroundings, and then they set off. They had to walk, since Silvis couldn't bring the Sapphire Mando with him on his bike. They soon arrived at the paintball field, where they hoped Ghast would be. They snuck around the paintball field and to the woods around it.

"Alright, what do we do now?" Silvis asked Junior.

"Let's wait for a moment to see if Ghast or any other Wild Cards are here, then we can execute the plan," Junior instructed.

"Alright." Silvis found a spot behind a large bush where it was quiet, so he could hear if anyone other than his friends were nearby. He lifted the Sapphire Mando and put it on his chin. He put the bow on top of the E string, ready to start playing when he was supposed to.

After waiting for a few minutes, Silvis still hadn't heard anything.

Pop! Something whizzed through the air.

Splat!

That must be Junior, Willow, and Bear shooting the confetti blasters.

"Huh?" a voice, probably not one of his friends, said.

I knew it! There are Wild Cards here! Silvis thought it was odd that he was excited, since a few days ago, he would've been extremely scared of a Wild Card being near him. Footsteps scattered Silvis's way. Through the bush, he saw two Wild Cards walking through the woods, looking for the source of all the noise.

Whizzzzz! Three confetti blaster pellets hit the Wild Cards. They screamed in pain and ran away.

"What?" a loud voice grumbled from a distance.

That must be Ghast. This is my chance.

Footsteps rushed towards him.

"Who's there?" the voice, probably Ghast's, grumbled.

Splat! The noise from the confetti blaster was close by, confetti hitting the tree next to him.

Uh oh. They tried to distract Ghast, but instead they sent him my way.

Ghast ran towards the bush Silvis was in. Silvis ran off.

"Hey! Get back here, boy!" Ghast screamed. Three Wild Cards appeared from a bush behind Ghast. Silvis immediately began playing the Sapphire Mando, charging up the power, while also running for his life.

Three pellets whizzed through the air and hit the Wild Cards. Silvis turned around to see Ghast rushing his way while the Wild Cards screamed in pain. *Thanks, guys!* thought Silvis, glad his friends had confetti-blasted the Wild Cards.

There was a small river a couple feet away; maybe he could somehow make Ghast fall in it. Silvis ran closer and closer to the river. When Ghast made it to the river, he tried to grab Silvis. But Silvis played a long E note straight at him, and a small but powerful beam of electricity blasted Ghast across the river and into a pile of leaves on the other side.

I did it. Ghast is unconscious. I did it!

"Are there any more?" called Silvis, turning in a circle, ready to strike.

"Nope," said Bear.

Silvis, Junior, Willow, and Bear spent half an hour taking Ghast's unconscious body to the chief of the Hillstretch Police Department's house, who lived in their neighborhood. According to Bear, the power that was blasted into

Ghast was so extreme that he would probably be unconscious for the rest of the day. Junior quickly jotted down something on a sticky note and stuck it on Ghast's mask.

They were about to leave when Willow said, "Wait! There's something in his pocket. Do you think it's a clue?"

Sure enough, there was a corner of a piece of paper sticking out of Ghast's front pants pocket. Junior leaned down and picked it up. He unfolded the note, and everyone leaned in to read it.

Hello, Ghast.
No one in this city knows what's going on. You have done just what I asked as your master. I am proud of what you have done. I have new orders for you.
Come to the base for them.
From your master, Mr. Williams

"WHAT?!" Silvis bellowed.

"There's no way ..." he said in shock.

"That's why he replaced you with Charlie! Because it was him all along!" said Silvis.

"I can't believe it," said Willow.

Junior started pacing. "It was him all along... Mr. Williams... he betrayed all of us. Why would he do this? He's been a great principal for fifteen years. And he's the leader of the YLO?"

"I can't believe it, either. Mr. Williams is the last person I thought would do this," said Silvis.

"We have to go now! Come on!" Junior ran toward the sidewalk.

"What? Where?" said Bear.

"To confront Mr. Williams! If we're lucky, he'll still be at school!"

"Maybe we should split up," said Bear. "That way, if someone gets caught, the others can save them."

"Good idea," said Junior. "Silvis, you come with me. Bear, do you mind staying with Willow? You can go to—"

"My house," said Silvis. "Polo, my pet ape, will make you dinner."

"Thanks," said Willow, and then she and Bear ran towards Silvis's house.

"Let's go!" said Junior, breaking into a run. Silvis followed. I wish I had my bike, he thought.

"Oh, hey, guys!" someone said.

They all stopped. It was Ghost.

"Hey, Ghost," Silvis replied.

"It's been a while since I've seen you," said Ghost, approaching Silvis for a hug. "You've barely come to recess at school."

Why is he hugging me? Kinda weird.

Ghost gave Junior a hug, too. "Sorry, Ghost, but we really need to get going," said Junior, squirming away.

"Why?" said Ghost.

"Well, we think we just found out who the Wild Card boss is!" said Silvis.

"Really? Who is it?"

"I'll tell you after we come back," said Junior.

Ghost kicked the ground. "Ugh, I wish I could come with you, but I'm on my way to visit my grandma."

Junior shrugged, already walking away. "Next time."

"Wait, just tell me something, at least. Are they an adult or a kid?" said Ghost.

"Adult," said Silvis.

"Are you sure they're the Master?"

"Uh, we have pretty good proof," said Junior.

"Hm, okay. You shouldn't underestimate kids. They can be very smart, like you, Junior."

"That's true. Alright, bye!" Junior said, and the four of them bolted toward the school.

The front gates were closed, so they had to climb over them. Then, they ran towards the office, where Mr. Williams would hopefully be.

Silvis knocked on the office door a few times. A moment later, Mr. Williams opened the door, looking down at them with a smile.

"Hello, boys!" Mr. Williams greeted. "You shouldn't have climbed over the gates when they were closed. But what brings you here?"

"Hey, Mr. Williams, we have something important to talk to you about, can we talk inside?" Junior requested.

"Absolutely!" Mr. Williams said cheerfully.

Mr. Williams led them to his office, where a round, wooden table and five chairs were set up. Silvis and Junior sat on chairs facing the door, and Mr. Williams sat on a chair on the other side.

"So," Mr. Williams began. "What is it that you need?"

"Something that has already been answered," Junior replied dramatically. "So, tell me, Mr. Williams, why you started the Griefings and why you're the leader of the YLO."

"I'm afraid I don't understand?"

"Playing dumb isn't gonna help you, sir. Surprised, aren't you? Two boys were able to crack the case of the Griefings and find out who was behind all of it? Yes, it can be done, and it has been done. We have proof, as well." Junior unzipped his backpack and took out the letter that Mr. Williams had sent to Ghast.

Mr. Williams eyed the letter warily.

We came way too unprepared. What if he attacks us all of a sudden? He is the Wild Card Master, after all.

"So, I see you have done it. You have cracked the case and found me, the one behind it all." His voice sounded far too simple to Silvis. Something wasn't right.

"Why did you do it? Why would you do it?" said Junior.

"Those, my friend, are questions I'm afraid I can't answer," said Mr. Williams.

"You might want to answer them now, or you'll be telling them to the cops when you're being detained," said Junior.

"How did you figure it out?"

"I know you're stalling and it's not gonna work." Junior unzipped his backpack and took out his computer. "Silvis, keep an eye on him."

Silvis nodded and watched Mr. Williams while also watching Junior. Once

Junior turned on his computer, he clicked on the calling icon on the taskbar and typed in the numbers nine-one-one, the emergency services number, and he pressed "search." There was the number and an icon that said "dial". Junior hovered his mouse over the dial icon, ready to click it.

Junior turned around his computer and showed it to Mr. Williams. "I will click the button if you don't cooperate," he said. "So you better give me the answers I want!"

A phone started ringing. Mr. Williams took his phone out of his pocket. "Don't you touch that phone!" Junior ordered. "Show me who's calling you or I will call the cops!"

Mr. Williams hesitated for a moment, then turned around his phone. It was a call from "The Master."

"What?" Silvis gasped.

"That's right," Mr. Williams said. "I'm not the Master."

"Then who is? You have to tell us now or I'll call the police!" said Junior.

"I can't. He'll kill me!"

"You have to tell us! We'll find a solution, and everyone will be safe," Silvis said.

Suddenly, strong hands grabbed Silvis. He struggled trying to free himself, but the captor was too strong. He looked the other way to see a tall Wild Card grabbing Junior. He hadn't even heard them come into the office! The Wild Card whipped the letter of proof out of Junior's hand, walked to Mr. Williams, and gave it to him.

"Hey! Let us go!" Silvis protested hopelessly. *We're dead, aren't we? And there's nothing we can do.*

"I'm sorry, boys," said Mr. Williams. "But I'm going to have to ask you to leave before I take more drastic measures."

Silvis and Junior were pulled out of the office by the Wild Cards, who blocked every attempt to break free the boys tried. The Wild Cards pulled the gates open and shoved Silvis and Junior onto the street, then immediately shut and locked the gates.

"Don't come back! You know what'll happen!" one of the Wild Cards hissed.

That wasn't so bad. Mr. Williams just kicked us out. I'm glad he's not actually the Master.

"Urgh! We were so close. Who's the Master, then?" said Junior.

"I don't know," said Silvis. "I'm just glad they let us go."

The heavy wind, the pouring rain, and the crackling thunder delayed Silvis and Junior's trip even more than it already was with them being on foot, but eventually, they made it back to Silvis's house.

Silvis opened the door and stepped inside. He took off his coat and threw it on the ground.

"Who's there?" Bear's voice thundered from up the stairs.

"Us! Me and Junior!" Silvis replied.

Bear and Willow came downstairs, Polo close behind.

Junior explained to Bear and Willow everything that happened, and Silvis chimed in for some parts. When they were done, Bear and Willow seemed quite shocked.

"That was our chance. We could've found out who the Master really was!" Junior complained.

"Well, lucky for us, we have another chance," Willow gushed.

"What do you mean?" Silvis asked.

"Polo and I have been working on something. We found out that the YLO have case files, and we just hacked the system and found them. I'm hoping that we might be able to find some good information from this."

"Wait, what? You know how to hack?"

"Well, it's a skill I usually never use, but it's definitely helping right now."

Silvis was quite surprised that Willow was a hacker, but at the same time, he wasn't. It seemed like something that matched the kind of person Willow was: mysterious and helpful.

"C'mon, my computer's upstairs," said Willow. Everyone followed her to the spare bedroom where she was working.

On Willow's computer were a bunch of different photos and blurbs about the crimes the YLO had committed.

"Well, we gotta work with what we have. Everyone, look for any clues," Junior instructed them.

Silvis examined the information on the computer. Many of the photos were old, from decades before the present time. One of the pictures was a picture of the YLO escaping a building after a murder and another was after a robbery. A lot of it was old, as the YLO's main reign of terror was long ago. The YLO were broken up and mostly destroyed after Junior's father found out where their main base was. That's why they hate Bear and Junior so much. Their father ended most of the YLO's days of glory.

Silvis continued to scan the photos until something caught his eye. It was the latest picture. It was from the year 2016, and it showed a picture of the YLO after kidnapping a board member of a popular car company. The YLO wore morph suits, ski masks, and vests. The shoulders of their vests had "YLO" in white letters on them. Something about it was familiar, as if he had seen it before. Then it struck him. Silvis had once seen Ghost wearing the same vest the night he played chess at Junior's house.

Ghost. His friend Ghost.

It can't be. Is Ghost a Wild Card?

"Guys, you need to see this," Silvis called. He pointed at the part of the vest that said "YLO." "Ghost wore this to school once. I'm a hundred percent sure."

"Wait, you mean Ghost, like your friend Ghost?" Bear asked.

"Yes, him."

"Oh yeah, he did. I remember. But we all trust Ghost," Willow said. "It must be a coincidence."

"Wait a minute," Junior said. "This motorcycle... it looks exactly like Ghost's!" Junior pointed to a motorcycle in one of the pictures. "And the caption says that the bike was created two hundred years ago by a YLO leader. Once a leader dies, the new leader gets the bike."

"Does that mean that... well, that Ghost is the leader of the YLO?" Silvis asked.

"Maybe," said Junior. "And look, this caption says that the YLO leaders have a key that opens a special room in the Hillstretch City Community House. The room has a bunch of ammo and other supplies. Isn't that what you found, Silvis?"

"Yes! Me and Polo had that key, but when Ghost rescued us, the key disappeared ... because he must've taken it!"

"All the clues perfectly align together! We've found the Wild Card Master!"

said Junior, smiling.

"Are you sure?" said Willow. "I can't believe it."

It took Silvis a while to process the news. *Ghost? Our friend was a traitor all along? How could he possibly do such a thing? He must've been using us. He knew about Junior being a good detective, so he tried to set Junior off or find a way to destroy him. Ghost is the mastermind behind the Griefings. That was why he's always busy and taking notes during recess.*

The only question that Silvis was still dying to know was why? *Why would Ghost do it?* He would have to find out.

CHAPTER 13
MEETING

The next day, Silvis awoke looking forward to going to the talent show, which was starting at 7:30. All day at school, he was unable to get his mind off the case. Junior had decided that they shouldn't act yet, so Silvis had to pretend like he was excited to see Ghost instead of angry that Ghost was a traitor and the leader of an evil organization. That night, Bear, Willow, and Junior met at Silvis' house for a meeting before they set off on their mission.

This could be the day that we stop him and end everything. We have to stop the Wild Cards, once and for all, before they make another move.

"Guys! Guys!" Junior called from down the stairs as he walked into Silvis' house. "You gotta see this!"

Junior was wearing a suit and tie and was drenched from the rain. "Silvis! Ghost sent me a letter; it was outside my house! He wants to have a meeting with all of us at his house and talk about some 'important matters,' as he said. It's probably a trap, but we have to go! We could capture him!"

Junior told the news to Bear and Willow, and they were soon ready to go. Everyone packed a confetti blaster and Silvis packed the Sapphire Mando. They walked to Ghost's house together.

Within minutes they arrived. The large two-story house was massive, painted gray, with a couple of windows and gates towards the entrance that were open.

"Alright," Junior began. "Get ready and expect anything."

Junior rang the doorbell. A few moments later, Ghost appeared at the door. "Hello!" he said. "Come in, come in and please take off your shoes!"

They all slipped off their shoes and stepped inside.

"Hey, Ghost! Great to see you," Silvis said, trying to sound as enthusiastic as possible. "This is a real nice house!"

"Thanks. Is that a violin?"

He won't suspect anything, will he? "Yeah, I'm performing in the talent show."

"Cool," said Ghost.

Everyone said hi, and then Ghost led them up the stairs. "This room," Ghost said, pointing to a door. He opened it, and there was a table with four chairs on one side and one chair on the other side. "Take a seat. There's no time to waste. This has been a tough investigation, but now I've heard from Silvis that you've found the Wild Card Master. That's what sparked an idea of meeting with all of you. So, let's get this straight, what's going on?"

"Well, it's pretty complicated, but we thought Mr. Williams was the Wild Card Master. Turns out, it's not him. We're still trying to figure out who," Silvis lied. He wasn't sure if that was the best answer, but it was too late to change it.

"So, you're still trying to find out who the Master is?" Ghost asked.

"Exactly," Silvis replied, gritting his teeth. *He's right there. Why can't we just all attack him at once? He wouldn't stand a chance!* Silvis then realized that Ghost must be much too smart to be unprepared.

"So, how are we gonna do this?" Ghost asked.

"What do you mean?" Junior said.

"Like, how are we gonna find out who it is?"

"I'm not sure. There are many things we can do, though," said Junior.

A moment later, two boys walked into the room carrying a tray of five cups of water. They gave everyone a cup and then left the room.

"Who are they?" Silvis asked.

"They work for me. They used to work for my dad," Ghost explained.

Work for him? He's only twelve! Silvis raised his cup to his lips and sipped some water.

"So, the water was unnecessary," said Ghost.

"Why?" said Willow.

"Because you won't be needing it anymore."

What does he mean—

Silvis had no time to think. Arms grasped hold of him and tied his hands together. He struggled to free himself, but nothing happened. Then they tied his legs to the wooden chair he was on. He looked to his left to see all three of his friends getting tied up as well.

"Argh! What's going on?" Willow demanded as she tried to escape the strong grip that was holding her.

"Ghost! You little—" Junior began, but the Wild Card tying him up covered his mouth.

"Such a shame," Ghost mocked, sounding just like a villain from an action movie. "You really had to get rid of Ghast."

"You won't hold us here for long! You can't stop us!" Silvis hissed.

Ghost chuckled loudly. "I'd like to see you try to escape."

"Silvis, calm down. None of that is gonna help you," Bear advised.

"Yes, listen to the big boy. Now, hush, child, while I present my epic villain speech."

"You sure are doing a good job being one, but let's be honest, I don't think a good villain would say that," Silvis joked.

"Shut up!" Ghost bellowed.

Silvis glared at Ghost miserably. He wished he could punch Ghost in the face until his knuckles bled, but there was nothing he could do. He had lost. He had to accept defeat.

"You fools have been so hard to get rid of, I'll admit it," Ghost said. "But because of your stupidity, I have you here. Now, I can finally execute my plan."

"What do you mean?" Junior asked. "Were the Griefings not enough for you?"

"Ah, yes. That's the question I want to hear. You see, 'detective', the Griefings were never what I wanted. It was simply a distraction, so I could produce my main plan, which is much worse."

Silvis' insides shivered. *What could possibly be worse than the Griefings?*

"But that's another topic," Ghost continued. "First, we have to start from the beginning. There is so much you guys don't know. You should be glad I'm explaining everything before I kill you."

"You won't kill us without a fight," Silvis growled.

"Anyways, it all started with the YLO. Three-hundred-fifty years ago, a criminal organization started. Using the power of its ultimate weapon, they were the best and the most powerful. No one ever came in their way or tried stopping them. If they did, the result would be death. But this organization was started by one half of a family that decided to name it 'Your Local Organization', YLO for short. The half of the family that created the YLO thrived, while the other half failed. They did all they could to stop the YLO, but they failed every time. The only solution was to make another weapon just like the YLO's, one that could fight back."

Ghost stopped, walked over to Silvis, and then went to the wall behind Silvis, where the case of Silvis' violin was. He picked it up and unzipped it, then pulled out the Sapphire Mando. "And that weapon happens to be right here, the Sapphire Mando, created by Goliath Mando in the year 1650 as a last resort to fight against the YLO. Now, it lies in my hands, and I can do anything with it."

"You wouldn't dare—" Junior said. "Wait, how do you know about the Sapphire Mando?"

"Because it is my family's history. Now, let me go back to a few years ago. My father died of liver cancer and I, as a seven-year-old boy, was forced to take over the YLO at a young age. My father named me Ghost, which is a code name, but my brother was killed by the police after they found out his real name. So, my dad made my name a code name itself. He named his best soldier, Ghast, the YLO General, after me as a promise that Ghast would always care for me when I called upon his help. To the public, it seemed like we wanted to commit crime simply for our own benefit, but our real goal all along was to gain as much power as possible. So that's what I did.

"After I found YLO's secret weapon, I used it to reconnect us and become stronger. My main goal was to take over Hillstretch City. I spent five years planning for the moment: the Griefings. At one point, Bear came close to stopping us, but we took care of that." Ghost glared at Bear, who glared back.

Ghost continued, "I formed an army of kids, when I could've had a much stronger one consisting of powerful grown adults. But instead I chose kids, so that I could dig in from the inside, get the information I need, and most of all, because no one would ever suspect kids to be the ones behind it. The Griefings were simply a distraction. A distraction that broke the whole city apart and made everyone scared. That was just what I needed, so, while my real plan was being worked on, people were trying to figure out the Griefings while I could slowly find a solution to taking over this city. And that is what I did. You guys investigated the Griefings. We had a few close calls, like when Silvis found the key to our secret room in the Community House, and I had to order an adult Wild Card to chase him and his dumb ape in and SUV."

"That was your doing? But you rescued us!" cried Silvis.

"It's called lying, Silvis. I pretended to be on your side so you would trust me. Anyway, I stayed informed on the case and only gave you the information I wanted you to have. Eventually, your investigation led you to me and my plan, after you found me on the YLO case files."

"What? How do you know that?" Bear asked.

"Because I saw Silvis when he and Junior were on the way to Mr. Williams's office. I slipped a tiny audio recorder on him. I heard everything. And I decided it was officially time to get rid of you for good."

Silvis was surprised by how smart Ghost was. *He put an audio recorder on me and heard everything about the case files and our confrontation with Mr. Williams! That's genius!*

"And so now, my final stage of the plan before I take over this city: the talent show. But before I get to that, Silvis, do you know why you have the Sapphire Mando?"

"No, I don't," Silvis answered.

"You, Silvis, are the descendant of Goliath Mando, the creator of the Sapphire Mando."

"WHAT?!" Silvis bellowed.

"Yes, I am not kidding. But this may surprise you even more."

"What? There's no way anything is more surprising than me being the descendant of—"

"You are my cousin, Silvis," Ghost interrupted.

"No way."

"Yes way. I chose this town to conquer because of you. You come from the other side of our family, the horrible good side that has been in the YLO's way for so many years. And now, I can finally get revenge on my cousin and end the good side of the family—except this time, I'll finish you properly, unlike the way my father got rid of your parents."

Silvis' head was hurting like crazy, and he was getting dizzy. This was too much to take in. "W-what? My mother and father? You know what happened to them?"

"Yes, I sure do."

"W-what?"

"Your parents are from the good side of our family. They spent their whole life trying to stop the YLO, and they never used the Sapphire Mando that was rightfully theirs. They feared that if the YLO got the Sapphire Mando, it would be chaos. When the YLO was robbing a bank, they tried to stop them but were unsuccessful and had to run away. But there were security cameras everywhere and the YLO were witnesses. So, my dad framed your parents for robbing the bank and they were arrested."

"They—they what?"

"Yes, Silvis. Believe it or not, they were arrested."

They've been in prison the whole time, rotting in there, all because of the YLO. Silvis was surprised and enraged. He wanted to destroy all the Wild Cards. "Oh, Silvis. You won't be seeing your parents when they finally come home. Another twenty years, I think?" Ghost taunted.

"Anyways," Ghost continued. "The talent show. Ah, yes, the talent show. I'm going to raid the talent show with my secret weapon. Oh, all the hostages I'll have! This is so great! They won't see it coming. The city will be forced to surrender to me. As my Wild Cards expand, I can create a new, better army that will spread through the city and conquer."

"And what are you gonna do with the Sapphire Mando?" Silvis asked. "And what's your secret weapon?"

"Oh, Silvis. You probably think the Sapphire Mando is only famous for its sound. Well, three-hundred-fifty years ago, everyone knew about it, and everyone knew about its powers. The Sapphire Mando's sound might be great, but it was really famous for its electric beam. The power was worth millions, but the Mandos had to make it a secret, as it was too dangerous having everyone in Italy know about it. So, people just thought it was a great violin. Goliath learned to control it, so only when he wanted to use its power would he make it fire."

Wow. This is just too much information. My head is hurting and I hate this.

"As for your other question, Silvis, the answer is right here." Ghost walked over to a cabinet that had strong silver chains and five different locks. He laid his thumb on one of the locks, and suddenly, all the locks unlocked and chains fell down.

"Whoa," Silvis muttered.

Ghost opened the cabinet. Inside was a violin case that looked just like the Sapphire Mando's. Ghost unzipped the case and pulled out a midnight black violin with bright orange strings. Something about it was familiar.

"Wait a minute..." Silvis said. "Is that the lost Model 21 violin?"

Ghost nodded. "It's not like your stupid copy of a violin. This bad boy was created by the creator of the YLO. It's coated in a thin layer of extremely rare obsidian and the strings are made of orange sapphire. This was the inspiration of the Sapphire Mando. The Model 21 isn't its real name, either. It's actually called the Obsidian Bandit."

"Holy crap. That thing has been lost for centuries," Silvis said.

"It was never lost, just the property of the YLO. It's basically the same as the Sapphire Mando, although more powerful, since it was created first," Ghost explained.

"I knew it!" Junior blurted.

"Knew what?" Ghost asked.

"That the Wild Cards have another violin just like the Sapphire Mando. That was my theory."

"Well, good for you, but I don't care." Ghost turned to Silvis and grabbed the Sapphire Mando from the couch he had placed it on. He stood up and stuck the Sapphire Mando in front of Silvis' face.

"So, Silvis. While my dad and all the other YLO leaders would have used this violin for extra power, I don't need this cursed object of treason," Ghost said.

"What do you mean?" Silvis asked. "What are you gonna do?"

Ghost laughed like a maniac and then set down the Sapphire Mando and grabbed the Obsidian Bandit. He put it into position on his shoulder and took the bow out of the case. He played a beautiful but extremely quick tune on the violin.

I hope he's not charging it up to kill us.

"You fool, Silvis," Ghost said. "There is so much you don't know about the Sapphire Mando. I have mastered it, while you probably have no idea how to control it."

Ghost played a long A note, and a burst of orange electricity shot out of the scroll of the Obsidian Bandit, headed straight towards Silvis.

This is it. I guess this is what death feels like.

The beam blasted right into Silvis' chest. There was a searing, sensational pain all over Silvis' body, one like he had never felt before. The pain stung, worse than anything he could imagine. Silvis tried to scream out or comfort himself somehow, but he couldn't move a muscle. He was paralyzed, and all he could do was blink and stare at Ghost. From the corner of his eyes, Silvis saw his friends gazing at him in horror. There was nothing they he could do.

"I can do many things. I have mastered this weapon, and right now, I am the most powerful person in this city. For your information," he said, turning his head to the others, "I just paralyzed him. I can choose to shoot a beam, paralyze, even stun. There's no one getting in my way."

"What are you gonna do?" Willow asked.

"Oh, boy. Now for the fun part." Ghost smiled and set down the Obsidian Bandit. He picked up the Sapphire Mando and opened the glass doors at the fireplace. Silvis knew exactly what was going to happen next. "You can watch your precious little weapon burn." Ghost threw the Sapphire Mando into the flames and then quickly closed the glass doors.

No. This isn't happening right now. The old, antique, legendary, powerful, price-less violin was burning. Silvis' only hope was gone. The city's only hope, the only thing that could save it. Silvis stared at the burning violin, helpless. Ghost cackled with evil laughter. Silvis got extremely drowsy, and a moment later, everything went black as he passed out.

•

"Silvis!" a voice yelled. "Get up! The talent show is starting in only twenty minutes, we gotta hurry!"

Silvis' eyes flickered open, and he saw Junior, Bear, and Willow standing in front of him.

"Yeah. Whatever you say, man," Silvis replied drowsily. Junior whacked him in the face. "Wait, what? How are you guys free?"

"Ghost and the Wild Cards went to the talent show, like, ten minutes ago. We untied ourselves and escaped and also broke his table in the process, but who cares? We are not going down without a fight today," Bear answered, untying Silvis' arms and legs.

Silvis looked around. He was in another completely empty room that had only a tiny bit of light coming from a small lamp on the ground.

"Where am I? This isn't where I was before! And the Sapphire Mando! What's happened?"

"Calm down, Silvis, everything's gonna be fine," Willow said.

"Ghost moved you to another room after you passed out," Bear said. "They stole all of our weapons, too."

"What do we do now?" Silvis asked, thinking of the Sapphire Mando, which was probably a lump of ash.

"We're gonna go to the talent show and do our best to stop Ghost, even if we die trying," Junior said.

CHAPTER 14

TALENT SHOW

Their plan was quite simple: Since Bear knew how to drive and Junior's dad's old car was still in the garage, they were going to drive to the talent show to avoid Wild Cards. The four of them bolted to Junior's house for the car.

"Is the list safe?" Silvis asked cautiously when they arrived.

"Yup," Junior replied. In Ghost's house, they had found a huge list that showed all the Wild Card kids and some adults and their status (their positions, whether they were forced into being a Wild Card or not, whether they were still a Wild Card, and so on). This list was just what they needed, but it wouldn't be any use at all if they didn't stop Ghost.

Everyone piled into the car while Bear grabbed the keys from a hook on the wall. He got the car started and then drove towards the school. "I think we'll be safe from any Wild Cards in the car," said Bear.

Not even a minute later, Silvis, who was in the back seat with Willow, saw ten Wild Cards on motorcycles, zooming towards them.

"We are definitely not safe," he said, panic rising in his voice.

Oh, great, we are gonna die. No, Silvis, we definitely are not going to die, so stop being so negative!

The fleet of motorcycles got closer and closer to them. Bear was forced to do different maneuvers. He charged straight towards a ditch, with the motorcycles zooming right behind him, then quickly did a sharp left. The Wild Cards didn't see it coming, and two of them fell straight into it.

"Yes!" Silvis cheered. "This is just like a chase scene in a movie!"

"Is that what you're thinking about?" Willow said, her voice shaking. "We're all gonna die right now! There are still eight more!"

Silvis heard Bear swear under his breath in annoyance.

After some more maneuvers and tricks, there were only three more Wild Cards chasing them. "I've had enough," Bear said. "It's time to put an end to this. Hold on tight, 'cause this is gonna be real rough."

Bear drove for a bit longer until they were on a very wide road, and he suddenly took a turn. Although he lost a lot of speed and momentum, he quickly gained it back as he charged towards the three Wild Cards, who were riding on their motorcycles alongside them.

"I have a bad feeling about this," Silvis said.

The car rammed the motorcycles, making the whole car shake. His head jerked forward, and the three Wild Cards fell off the motorcycles, flying a few feet in the air and slamming onto the ground.

"Dang, that must hurt," Willow said. "But that was super sick!"

Bear stopped the car and Junior got out.

"What's he doing?" Silvis asked.

Junior walked over to the injured Wild Cards lying on the ground and took out a few pieces of rope. He tied up all the Wild Cards' arms and legs and got back into the car. "It won't be long before more of them come," Junior said.

"That's why we gotta get to the talent show now," Bear replied. He revved the engine and drove towards the school. "That Ghost guy may be a mastermind, but he's pretty stupid to tell us his entire plan."

"Yeah, that's because he didn't expect us to escape. And he probably thinks that even if we did, we wouldn't be able to do anything," Junior answered. Well, without the Sapphire Mando, we probably can't do anything, Silvis added to himself.

"Yeah, well, he made the wrong decision to mess with the... uh..." Willow said. "Guys, we don't have a team name."

"We don't need a team name, that's lame," Silvis said.

"You have my support on that," Junior said.

"Aw, come on," Willow complained in defeat. "Bear? What about you?"

"I'm not becoming a part of this," Bear said.

The five of them finally arrived at the multi-purpose room parking lot. Everyone exited the car and walked towards the multi-purpose room.

"What's the plan? Do we even have a plan?" Silvis asked.

"No, I'm afraid not," Junior answered.

"Darn it! Why don't we have a plan?"

"'Cause we didn't have any time," Junior replied. "But we can come up with a quick one now."

"Um, how quick?" Bear asked skeptically.

"We basically need to find a way to get backstage. I think there's a door at the back of the multi-purpose room that can take us there. And then when Ghost has taken control, we strike."

"With what? We don't have any weapons," Silvis said.

"We don't need weapons. We all promised to fight no matter what the cost, even if it's our lives. We use ourselves."

Silvis wanted to argue, but he knew Junior was right. There was no time to get weapons. They were going to have to fight with their bodies.

Unlike other schools, Hillstretch Elementary's multi-purpose room was huge. This was mainly because the stage was used often and the school needed a lot of space, due to the large number of students. There was a huge backstage and a lot of space on the ground for the audience to watch.

The kids crept into the multi-purpose room and through the door at the back. They were in a storage room that had different boxes and costumes with labels. They looked around the dusty room, but there was nothing useful. Bear walked up to the door and slowly opened it. Silvis saw him peek out to see if anyone was near.

"All clear," Bear confirmed. They slowly snuck out of the room and into a big hall. The lights were on, and they heard chatter coming from some of the rooms.

"Alright, ladies and gentlemen!" a familiar voice boomed, scaring all four of them.

"Is that Mr. Williams?" Bear asked.

"Yeah," Silvis replied, recognizing the voice.

"So the talent show must be starting now?" Willow asked.

"It's got to be," Junior answered. "Everyone, get ready."

They waited for some time as Mr. Williams talked to the audience. "And now, for our first contestants," Mr. Williams began dramatically.

From across the hall, they saw nine girls walking towards the stage wearing dresses. *The ballet girls I saw in the Community House!* Silvis thought to himself. Among those girls was Elly, who was leading them.

"Ladies and gentlemen, I present to you, the ballet girls!" Mr. Williams cheered as the girls entered the stage.

Silvis heard cheering and clapping from the audience. Then suddenly, a voice thundered above all, "Not before my performance!"

Silvis knew this was Ghost's voice.

Thump! He guessed the noise was Ghost getting onto the stage. The ballet girls screamed while the audience muttered in confusion.

"Such a vulnerable place. What a shame that you were the first contestants," Ghost said in his evil voice.

"Ghost?" Elly asked. "What are you doing here?"

"It'll all make sense in a second. Now, it's time for you and your girls to go to sleep."

"What do you mean?"

"NO!" Silvis bellowed. He ran through the hall, through the backstage area, and towards the stage.

"Silvis, wait!" Junior called.

Silvis heard the others chasing after him. Ignoring them, Silvis pushed the stage curtains aside, and when he saw Ghost, he immediately pounced on him. But Ghost was strong, much stronger than Silvis, and Ghost fought back. The two wrestled for thirty seconds, and then Bear, Willow, Junior joined in. Then five Wild Cards emerged from behind the curtains and surged towards them. The audience was yelling and screaming. Some people ran out of the multi-purpose room. *Where are the teachers? Why aren't they stopping this?* Silvis thought as he dodged Ghost's punch.

"AH! What is going on?!" Elly demanded in fear.

"Elly, don't worry!" Willow said desperately as she crawled away from the fight.

"What do you mean, don't worry?! What are all of you guys doing here with some huge guy, and what is Ghost doing?!"

"There's no time to explain! Can't you see the situation? Ghost is evil!" said Willow. She then dove back into the fighting.

Silvis, Junior, Bear, and Willow tried their best to fight off the Wild Cards, but one almost-adult and three eleven-year-olds weren't enough. To make matters worse, ten more Wild Cards emerged from the curtains, holding confetti blasters (most likely the ones Ghost had stolen from Junior) and ropes. They threatened Elly and the ballet girls with the confetti blasters while the others tied them up. The ballet girls screamed in fear, but then the Wild Cards taped their mouths shut. After that, the Wild Cards dropped their weapons and joined the battle with their bodies, as they couldn't shoot the confetti blasters without risking hitting other Wild Cards.

The ten Wild Cards grabbed the confetti blasters and aimed at Silvis, Junior, Willow, and Bear. There were too many of them. There was no way out. Silvis, Junior, Willow, and Bear had no choice but to accept defeat. They raised their hands and announced, "We surrender!"

"You have made the right choice," Ghost said. "You would've just died in a worse way if you continued."

What are we doing? We're letting them win! The whole city is gonna die! I can't give up!

Silvis was about to argue with the others, but then he saw something above his head moving very quickly through the curtains. It disappeared as fast as it came. Silvis looked around for it to come back, but there was nothing. *Just my imagination. Dealing with this case must've driven me crazy.*

"AHH!" one of the Wild Cards suddenly howled.

"OW!" another screamed.

Silvis saw two Wild Cards clutching their heads in pain, and then three more from behind him screamed at the same time.

"What's going on—OW!" Ghost shouted.

Has someone come to save us? But no, what's small enough for us to not be able to see it but also quick enough? Something popped into his head. There's no way...

But there was a way, because the unmistakable body of none other than Polo leapt off the giant curtains, jumped on a Wild Card's head, and punched him.

"GAH!" the Wild Card shrieked. "What is that?!"

Silvis forced himself not to smile. Polo came for us and now he's kicking butt.

Bear, Silvis, Willow, and Junior all seized the opportunity of Polo's distraction and pounced at different Wild Cards. Silvis's target happened to be Ghost. This is great, since I really want to knock some sense into Ghost, but also bad, since Ghost is way stronger than me.

"You messed up this time!" Ghost thundered. He threw a strong and swift punch at Silvis's face.

Crack! Silvis's nose burst with blood and seared with pain. Ghost had definitely broken his nose, and Silvis was furious. But Ghost didn't have any mercy, and he sent an extremely powerful roundhouse kick at Silvis's chest, sending Silvis falling onto the ground.

"Silvis!" Junior screamed. "I'm coming! I'm coming to help you—ow!"

Silvis could tell that his friends wanted to help him badly but couldn't, since they had their own enemies stopping them. Ghost jumped on Silvis and kept him pinned on the ground. Silvis landed a punch on Ghost's face, but it only stunned Ghost for a few seconds, which wasn't enough time for Silvis to escape Ghost's weight. Ghost was much stronger than he was, and he was doomed. Just when all hope seemed lost, a violin case slid across the stage floor. Silvis recognized it as the case of the Sapphire Mando. Didn't it burn? He set aside his confusion, eager for anything that could help. With a surge of power, he shoved Ghost off him and rushed towards the case. He quickly opened it, and inside was the Sapphire Mando, with lots of scorch marks and burnt-off diamond dust. The strings looked heavily damaged, too, but still playable enough to make a good sound.

Silvis grabbed the Sapphire Mando and the bow. As Ghost rushed towards him, he played a long E note. A beam of electricity hit Ghost right in the chest, but since Silvis hadn't charged up the zap, Ghost was only knocked back and stunned for a moment, quickly becoming fine again.

"Give me the case!" Ghost ordered one of his cronies. *Who is he talking to?* Silvis thought.

Silvis's question was answered when a hand stuck out from behind the curtain and slid the case of the Obsidian Bandit over to Ghost. Ghost quickly opened it and grabbed the Obsidian Bandit and the bow, ready to strike. He played a long G note while Silvis played a long A note.

Two beams of orange and blue electricity flew at each other and clashed. The beams made a small explosion, hitting two Wild Cards, who fell back a few feet. The Wild Cards charged towards Silvis, weapons raised. He shot a blast of electricity at them, and they all fell over.

"Wait!" Silvis yelled, but the Wild Cards didn't listen.

"Stop!" Ghost demanded. The Wild Cards stopped immediately. "Go guard the hostages. Let me hear what he has to say."

Silvis knew that even though he had the Sapphire Mando, it wouldn't be enough to stop the Obsidian Bandit and all the Wild Cards. But there was something he could do. A challenge.

"Ghost." Silvis stood proudly and valiantly. "I challenge you to a violin duel."

Ghost chuckled lightly. "Ah, a violin duel. One of those hasn't happened in centuries, but I will gladly accept."

He accepted. We actually have a chance.

"But you know nothing about the legendary violins. If you lose this, you are going to die," Ghost said.

At least I'll die a hero. "If I win, you and the Wild Cards must surrender and not come back. If you win, you can do whatever you want, and we shall surrender to you," Silvis said.

"Still accepted."

Silvis put his violin into position and so did Ghost. Silvis put his bow on the E string and waited for Ghost's signal.

"Three ... two ... one ..." Ghost counted. "Go!"

Silvis immediately began playing a tune very quickly and Ghost did the same. Silvis charged up the electricity and kept playing. *Come on, Silvis, you can do this.* He played as best as he could, but there was tension all over him. He couldn't resist the aching fear that the city would be taken over by the Wild Cards and that Ghost would kill him and his friends. He felt like he could do better, but no matter what he tried, the violin didn't sound any different.

Still playing his violin, Silvis thought he could outsmart Ghost and pull a fast one. He quickly played a long note, and a burst of electricity blasted towards Ghost. But Ghost was quick, and at the same time, he sent a blast back at Silvis. The two blasts of electricity flew at each other and clashed. Silvis expected them to explode, like the last time, but instead, the two beams were fighting each other, like a wizard wand fight. The beams continued to push each other, but none was winning—they were both just in the center.

Silvis played harder. His beam began overtaking Ghost's. *Yeah, that's it. You've got to win this.* Ghost played more, and the two beams continued to go back and forth.

The beams kept shifting. Sometimes Ghost's beam was winning, sometimes Silvis's beam was winning. It depended on greatness, skill, and consistency. Very quickly, Silvis used up more and more energy, getting more and more tired and more and more worried. All of this drew him away from success, and Ghost's beam pushed forward. It was soon only a foot away from the Sapphire Mando.

Both of our beams have been charged up so much and if that hits the Sapphire Mando, it's gonna destroy it and me. Silvis desperately tried to push the beam away, playing more and more, but all his attempts failed.

There's no point. I should just give up and accept my fate.

Silvis's whole body shook. He forced himself not to stop playing. He wasn't going to give up. *I won't. I can't. If I give up, then I'm just a coward.*

"Looks like someone's coming to an end!" Ghost cackled triumphantly. "You're a fool! You thought you could beat me! You, an orphan boy! You failed! You failed to defeat me!"

Ghost's taunting didn't make Silvis any less determined, but his words struck Silvis. *He said I failed. But why? Why did I fail? I know he's better than me at almost everything, but what makes him so much better at greatness, skill, and consistency? He might've mastered how to control the Obsidian Bandit, but that doesn't give him too much of an advantage.*

But then Silvis realized it. Ghost wasn't full of tension and fear. He was confident and fearless. *Confident and fearless. Courageous. I have to be courageous. I have to actually believe in myself.*

Silvis took a deep breath and let out the fear in him. *You can do this! You are Silvis Wren, the descendant of Goliath Mando! You are strong and courageous!*

Silvis closed his eyes and played with all the remaining energy he had. More and more, the sound improved. Soon, Silvis was in a trance. He played without even having to pay attention, but he just focused on his goal and the beauty of his music. Although his eyes were closed and he couldn't see, he could tell that the Sapphire Mando's beam was making progress.

"WHAT!" Ghost thundered. "HOW IS THIS POSSIBLE?!"

Silvis slowly opened his eyes. Ghost was yelling in anger as Silvis's beam got closer and closer to him.

"YOU WILL GO DOWN WITH ME, TRAITOR!" Ghost shrieked. There was terror in his eyes, though. He knew he had lost.

A moment later, with a burst of energy, Silvis's beam struck the Obsidian Bandit.

It all happened in what felt like a second. The Obsidian Bandit immediately blew up, pieces of the ancient obsidian and wood flying everywhere, but the beam sliced right through it and hit Ghost in the chest. The explosion also hit Mr. Williams, who was right next to Ghost and had been trying to stop the fighting. Ghost hardly had a second to scream, as the power of the Sapphire Mando's beam and the explosion of the Obsidian Bandit blew him a few feet in the air and sent him flying towards the wall.

Bang! Ghost hit the wall and then fell down onto the floor, unconscious. The audience that was still in the room cheered.

"Silvis!" Junior screamed in joy.

"You did it!" Willow exclaimed.

The Wild Cards were forced to stand down, since the deal was that they would have to surrender. A Wild Card began untying all the ballet girls. Once Elly was untied, she screamed, "I don't know what just happened, but that was awesome! You saved everyone!"

All five of Silvis's friends ran toward him, and he wanted to hug them all at once. But he had so little energy he couldn't even move.

The last things he heard were the audience's cheering and clapping and the sirens of police cars. The last thing he saw was the burnt-up, limp, and possibly lifeless body of Mr. Williams before everything went black.

CHAPTER 15

NEW DUTIES

Beep! Beep! The noise filled Silvis's ears. Silvis couldn't feel anything, and he didn't remember anything, either.

"Silvis?" a voice said softly.

"Silvis, are you okay?" another voice asked.

Something gently shook him, and his eyes began to open. Everything suddenly came back to him. The last thing he remembered was defeating the YLO and passing out.

Silvis looked around and saw a hospital room. There was a tube connecting his arm to an IV machine. That was what was beeping. He was wearing a hospital gown and an oxygen mask.

"I don't need all this stuff!" Silvis muttered. He pulled off the oxygen mask. To his right were all four of his friends, Junior, Willow, and Elly, but not Bear.

"Is Bear alright?" Silvis asked.

"Unfortunately, his arm is gonna have to be amputated," Junior answered in a sad voice.

"Oh."

"But it's okay, he's gonna get a mechanical arm!" Willow squealed.

"Oh, wow!" Silvis said.

"But what's more important is what you did," Elly added.

"You saved all of us from Ghost! We were so worried, Silvis, but you did it!" Junior cheered.

"I—I did," Silvis muttered to himself in disbelief. *I beat the YLO and saved everyone.*

"How'd you do it?" Junior asked, full of excitement. "You looked like you were about to die of exhaustion and Ghost's beam was almost at the Sapphire Mando! But then suddenly your beam just blasted forwards after you closed your eyes and—and you defeated him!"

Silvis explained the secret of how he defeated Ghost: "I was just being courageous and enjoying what I was doing, even though I was at the brink of death."

"Wow," Willow whispered. "I never thought courage could do any good."

"I didn't think so either, but look where it brought me. Look where it brought us! We were all brave enough to stand up against the YLO!" Silvis cheered joyfully.

"Uh, I don't think I was the brave one here," Elly pointed out. "I was tied up the whole time."

"Doesn't matter," Junior said. "Still brave."

"So, we're all friends?" Willow asked.

"How about friends forever?" Silvis suggested.

"Yes!" all the others said at once.

Junior turned to Elly. "Also, Elly, you don't need to pay me for solving Zak's—I mean Bear's—disappearance. I've been wanting to find my brother for so long, and you hiring me to find Zak was just what I needed to find Bear."

"Thanks, Junior," said Elly. "That's so nice. I'm happy that you solved Zak's case, and the Griefings."

"Yeah," said Willow. "You were right all along—they were connected."

Junior smiled. "I couldn't have done it without all of your help."

Then they all left while the doctors ran some tests on Silvis.

After an hour of being alone in his room, the door opened, and an extremely short figure walked in. Silvis sat up and saw Polo staring at him with a proud face. "You did it!" Polo said, smiling.

"Polo, you saved us. Were you the one who brought me the Sapphire Mando during the fight?"

Polo nodded. "When you guys went to visit Ghost's house and didn't come back after a while, I knew something was wrong. So I went to the house, broke in, and searched all the rooms. That's when I saw the Sapphire Mando in the fireplace and a list of Ghost's plans to go to the talent show. So, I took the Sapphire Mando out of the fireplace." Polo lifted his hand and showed Silvis a scorch mark.

"Yikes! Are you okay?"

"I'm fine. But anyways, I knew you guys would be going to the talent show, so I went there with the Sapphire Mando and gave it to you!"

Then Junior came back into the room. "There's lots of new information!" he cheered.

"What is it?" Silvis asked. He wanted to know very badly.

"First of all, Bear got his mechanical arm! But most importantly, I heard from the authorities that Ghost is in a coma in the hospital. The government has decided that he isn't fit to fight his case in court. They searched his house and found evidence of hundreds of crimes he has generated or made possible. His sentence will be twenty-five years in prison!"

Phew. Ghost is gone. Twenty-five years, though! That's crazy. But he deserves it.

"But there's more! We submitted Ghost's list of all the Wild Cards and the cops are currently detaining the ones who joined at their own will and interviewing the ones that were forced into the job, like Mr. Williams and Devin. The Wild Cards are gone, for now, at least. And the cops want to interview me, you, Willow, Elly, and Bear about the case. Lots of news channels, too!"

•

Once Silvis, Polo, and Junior left the hospital, there was a swarm of reporters and citizens wanting answers. The cops cleared the crowd. Willow, Elly, and Bear arrived, and then the cops interviewed everyone. Although Silvis was the one who had defeated Ghost and beat the YLO, he didn't want to be known for something like that and be famous for a detective's job. That's why he gave Junior almost all the credit for everything. Because of Junior, the case was solved. He was the real detective.

After the interview, news quickly spread that Junior was the kid detective that solved the case. The kids were interviewed by many reporters, and they were on TV for most of the interviews. Silvis told them the same things he told the cops, that Junior was the one who solved the case and he needed most of the credit.

Finally, when the interviews were done, Silvis set off to go to his house with Polo. Once they arrived, Silvis jumped onto his couch and began watching TV. He was exhausted, and so was Polo. Most of the news channels he watched were interviews with him and his friends, and one of the channels was the California Daily, his favorite channel and the most popular in the state. On all the channels, Junior was soon called "the famous kid detective".

Although he had rested the whole night after he had passed out, he was still tired, probably from the stress of all the obstacles in the case. But he had finally solved it, and more importantly, stopped it. This was just what Junior needed, too, as Junior was definitely going to become a very successful detective (he was already a famous kid detective).

Silvis fell asleep while watching TV. But his nice, relaxing sleep was interrupted by the doorbell ringing. It was probably one of his friends. But why would they come to see me? *Don't they have things to do, too? They were just on so many news channels and now they're all famous.*

Silvis groaned in annoyance and walked toward the door. He opened it without looking to see who his visitor was. At his front door was a familiar lady. Silvis took a step back, but then he realized who it was. The lady had long, red hair and green eyes, and she was wearing a winter coat and boots.

This was Silvis's mother, Whitney Wren.

"Mother?" Silvis asked in disbelief.

"Silvis!" Whitney shouted.

Silvis ran towards her and hugged her as tight as he could. Silvis could feel his mom's tears dripping onto his head and he formed tears too. *Mother is here. Mother is back.* A moment later, Polo joined in the hug. A tall man with brown, wavy hair and blue eyes joined as well. This was Silvis's dad, Mark Wren.

"Dad!" Silvis shouted in joy. "How are you—"

"Because of you, Silvis!" Whitney said. "You beat the YLO! You did it! I knew you could do it! And you, Polo! You helped him! Because of you, he beat Ghost!"

"That was very nice of you to give the credit to your detective friend. It was the right thing to do," Mark him.

"We're here because the cops found out that we were framed by the YLO, which I'm guessing you already know," Whitney explained.

"Yes, I do."

"The cops found proof in Ghost's house. We're free, and we'll never go back to jail again. And we've got our jobs back too! But unfortunately, the government came to the conclusion that the Sapphire Mando was too powerful, and so it was destroyed."

Silvis frowned. "I guess that makes sense. But I did love playing that violin, even without shooting electricity."

He told his parents all about everything that he and his friends did, starting from the beginning, when he got the card that entered him into the school from Willow, to the end, when he defeated Ghost. His parents also told him their story of chasing down the Wild Cards and getting framed.

In the end, everyone was proud of each other. *I can finally live a normal, happy life. I don't need to be famous. I just need my family.*

·

Silvis and his family adjusted to their new life. Silvis and his friends still had a lot to do, including telling the police a full detailed explanation of everything that had happened, from how he became part of the case to how it ended.
It was the first day of fall break, and Silvis and his friends were going to meet at Newberry Park for the first time since the day after the talent show. Silvis arrived last, but this time, none of his friends were annoyed; they just seemed happy to see him.

Although it was nearly winter, the day was quite sunny. They sat and lay on the lime green grass of the park's field. They talked and laughed, and Silvis caught them up on everything that had happened during the week. They also had sandwiches made by Willow's mom.

"The Sapphire Mando may be destroyed, but there's something else," Silvis said.

"What?" Junior asked.

Silvis grabbed the violin case he had brought with him and opened it. Inside was an old wooden violin. "It's called the Model 100, the hundredth violin created by Goliath Mando, my ancestor. Looks like a normal legendary violin, right?"

"Uh, I guess..." Elly said.

"Well, you're wrong!" He took the violin and bow out of the case. He put it into position and he began to play a beautiful tune.

"Wow! That sounds goooood!" Willow said.

"But you said it's not a normal legendary violin. It looks normal to me," said Elly.

"That's right," Silvis said. "Watch this." He flipped the small iron switch that was at the bottom of the violin. When he played, the strings turned a bright green color. "My mother and I worked on this during the week."

"That's awesome!" Willow cheered.

"But it has to be a secret. I only have it just in case something bad happens." He played a long G note, and a blast of green electricity hit a tree next to them and made a small hole.

"Hey, look what I found yesterday," said Junior, pulling something out of his pocket. It was a Wild Card from a deck of cards.

"That's the one I gave you at the beginning of the case!" said Elly.

Junior nodded. "Silvis, I never asked. Is this where you got the idea to call the YLO Wild Cards?"

"Yes, actually," said Silvis. "I think my card is somewhere in my basement. Why did you give those to us, Elly? It was so random."

Elly shrugged. "I got a card deck with two extra Wild Cards and I didn't know what to do with them. I just thought it would be kinda cool."

"Well, I'm glad you gave them to us," said Junior. "Now I'll remember this case forever."

"You'll remember the case forever? Will you remember us forever?" Silvis asked.

"Of course he will, dummy!" Willow said, hitting Silvis on the head with her sandwich. "Friends forever."

"Friends forever. I like the sound of that," Junior said.

"We all do," said Silvis, "and it's because we know that's what we're gonna be. Forever."